PRAISE FOR JESSICA DAY GEORGE'S

Tuesdays at the Castle *series*

"These kids are clever, as is George's lively adventure. May pique castle envy." —*Kirkus Reviews* on *Tuesdays at the Castle*

"This story puts an unexpected spin on the typical princess tale. Readers will root equally for crafty Celie and for her castle." —*Library Media Connection* on *Tuesdays at the Castle*

"There is a warmth here that is utterly irresistible."
—*BCCB* on *Tuesdays at the Castle*

"A charming, adventurous story with a spirit that will appeal to fans of Kate DiCamillo's *The Tale of Despereaux*. . . . *Tuesdays at the Castle* is all the more enjoyable for the intelligent, strong characters who dwell within its pages and castle walls." —*Shelf Awareness* on *Tuesdays at the Castle*

"There is plenty to charm readers in this second book in the series. . . . The Castle is a character in its own right, and readers will be fascinated to learn more about its history."
—*School Library Journal* on *New York Times*
bestselling *Wednesdays in the Tower*

BOOKS BY JESSICA DAY GEORGE

Dragon Slippers
Dragon Flight
Dragon Spear

Tuesdays at the Castle
Wednesdays in the Tower
Thursdays with the Crown
Fridays with the Wizards
Saturdays at Sea

Sun and Moon, Ice and Snow

Princess of the Midnight Ball
Princess of Glass
Princess of the Silver Woods

Silver in the Blood

The Rose Legacy

SATURDAYS at Sea

JESSICA DAY GEORGE

BLOOMSBURY

NEW YORK   LONDON   OXFORD   NEW DELHI   SYDNEY

First published in the United States of America in February 2017
by Bloomsbury Children's Books
Paperback edition published in February 2018
www.bloomsbury.com

Bloomsbury is a registered trademark of Bloomsbury Publishing Plc

For information about permission to reproduce selections from this book, write to
Permissions, Bloomsbury Children's Books, 1385 Broadway, New York, New York 10018
Bloomsbury books may be purchased for business or promotional use. For information on
bulk purchases please contact Macmillan Corporate and Premium Sales Department at
specialmarkets@macmillan.com

The Library of Congress has cataloged the hardcover edition as follows:
Names: George, Jessica Day, author.
Title: Saturdays at sea / by Jessica Day George.
Description: New York : Bloomsbury, 2017.
Summary: After traveling to the seaside kingdom of Lilah's betrothed prince, Lulath,
Celie and her companions are busy training griffins, enjoying wedding festivities,
and finishing construction of a grand ship built from parts of the Castle. But on
their maiden voyage, the Ship steers them far off course into uncharted waters.
Identifiers: LCCN 2016025589 (print) • LCCN 2016040684 (e-book)
ISBN 978-1-61963-957-7 (hardcover) • ISBN 978-1-61963-973-7 (e-book)
Subjects: | CYAC: Fairy tales. | Castles—Fiction. | Princesses—Fiction. |
Ocean travel—Fiction. | Magic—Fiction. | BISAC: JUVENILE FICTION /
Fantasy & Magic. | JUVENILE FICTION / Action & Adventure / General. |
JUVENILE FICTION / Family / Siblings.
Classification: LCC PZ8.G3295 Tu 2017 (print) | LCC PZ8.G3295 (e-book) |
DDC [Fic]—dc23
LC record available at https://lccn.loc.gov/2016025589

ISBN 978-1-68119-606-0 (paperback)

Book design by Donna Mark
Typeset by Newgen Knowledge Works (P) Ltd., Chennai, India
Printed and bound in the U.S.A. by Berryville Graphics Inc., Berryville, Virginia
2 4 6 8 10 9 7 5 3

Dedicated to all the readers
who have followed Celie and her Castle on their adventures:
you are all honorary griffin riders!

Chapter
1

❦

Celie stared across the courtyard of the Royal Palace of Grath. An endless sea of tiny dogs stared back.

"It's strangely terrifying," Rolf whispered.

"So many eyes," Celie whispered back.

The round, dark eyes of the countless dogs blinked moistly at them.

"I'm going to make a run for it," Rolf said.

"Don't you dare," Queen Celina murmured, putting a hand on his shoulder.

"They're just dogs," Lilah said. She sounded like she was trying to convince herself.

"Hello! Hello! Our tiny only darlings!" Prince Lulath of Grath danced forward into the endless expanse of dogs.

The little beasts went wild, yapping and leaping, prancing on their hind legs. Tails waved like ostrich-plume fans. Little pink tongues shot out and tried to lick

1

the prince's fluttering hands as Lulath attempted to pat every fluffy head.

"So *many* dogs," Rolf murmured.

"*Mio!* O *mio!* My son!"

The doors of the palace were flung open, and a tall man burst out of them. He was wearing a bright-yellow coat that dripped lace from cuffs and collar, scarlet trousers with gold embroidery up the sides, and gleaming black boots with red heels. His gray hair had been teased into a high arrangement of curls, and a golden crown nestled within the formation.

Celie and her family had plenty of time to observe this man's elaborate clothes and coiffure, as his grand flight from the palace doors was hampered by the dogs. Undaunted, arms still outstretched, he waded through them toward Lulath.

"*That's* the king of Grath?" Celie said in disbelief, though really, she shouldn't have been all that surprised. She'd known Lulath, who was also fond of small dogs and fancy clothes, for over a year now. But even Lulath didn't curl his straight blond hair.

"I feel ill," Lilah said.

Celie turned to look at her older sister, who was the entire reason they had traveled to Grath. Celie and Rolf and their mother were Lilah's escort as she met her future husband's family.

"You're fine," Rolf said. "You love dogs." He paused. "And Lulath," he added.

2

"I feel so underdressed," Queen Celina muttered, which startled Celie. She had never heard her mother sound uncertain about anything before.

A woman appeared in the doors of the palace.

"Oh, my," Celie said.

"We're *all* underdressed," Rolf said unhelpfully.

The woman almost filled the double doorway. Not that she herself was wide—in fact she was quite slim, and very tall. But her gown flowed out to each side of her in kilted layers of green and pink, trimmed with silver lace. The gown had a high flared collar of lace and a long floating cape behind it. Her hair was even higher and more elaborate than her husband's, and her crown was so encrusted with diamonds that the afternoon sun made it appear to shoot off sparks.

"O all my loves!" the woman cried, and she, too, began to make her slow progress through the dogs. "Oh, the silliness!" she finally cried, stopping in the middle in irritation.

She put two long fingers to her lips and whistled, a shockingly loud and piercing sound. The little dogs all turned and trotted obediently back inside the palace. The king looked at his queen as though he had never seen anything so amazing in his life. He exclaimed, in Grathian, that his wife was like a mighty goddess, which Celie translated for her mother.

The king and queen embraced their son, kissed his cheeks, and rejoiced in their native language that they were reunited at last. Lilah, who had studied Grathian with Rolf and Celie, made a gulping noise.

"They talk so *fast*," she whispered.

Her comment, of course, fell into the sudden silence as the king and queen released Lulath and turned expectantly to them. Lilah turned red to the roots of her shining dark hair.

Queen Celina stepped forward and graciously inclined her head. The king and queen of Grath did the same. Then Lilah and Celie both curtsied deeply, and Rolf bowed.

"O my father, O my mother," Lulath intoned in Sleynth. "I am being ever pleased to put before us the noble and beautiful queen, the very Celina of Sleyne!" He turned and flourished a hand toward his parents. "My very Queen Celina, here is being my noble father, my graceful mother, being King Kurlath and Queen Amatopeia."

They all bowed or curtsied, the Grathian couple with many more flourishes than their guests from Sleyne.

"O gracious mother and gracious father," Lulath continued. "I have so much the pleasure, truly so much, to also say to you, here is to be my bride, this vision of the vision, this Princess Delilah!"

Lilah curtsied even more deeply, and the Grathians curtsied and bowed back.

"And also it is being mine the delight to say to you, behold, here is a youngest brother and an only sister to my Delilah, who are as to me as dearest of friends and brother and sister also, the only Crown Prince Rolf, chosen by the very Castle Glower as the king the next, and the only Princess Cecelia, she for whom the Castle Glower and all the griffins have the greatest love!"

More curtsies, more bows, and then suddenly: hugging.

The king and queen of Grath, having finished their elaborate formal greetings, now rushed forward with arms outstretched. Queen Amatopeia swept Lilah up in a hug, literally lifting her off the ground and placing kisses on both her cheeks. King Kurlath gathered up Queen Celina, kissed her loudly on both cheeks, and then shook her a little, calling her his "queen sister." Then they switched, with the king hugging and kissing Lilah, the queen doing the same to Queen Celina, and then, to Celie's discomfort, turning their attention to herself and Rolf. Rolf and Celie soon found themselves enveloped in silk and lace and also lifted off the ground. The queen's kisses left sticky spots of lip rouge on Celie's cheeks, but she was pleased that the king's kisses were actually warm and dry. From the smacking noises she'd expected something a bit more moist.

"And now that is being the finish," King Kurlath announced. "We can be coming into the palace and having of food and comfort."

"How lovely," Queen Celina said.

They all began to move toward the doors of the palace, and servants started to appear out of other, smaller doors, to take care of the carriage and the luggage. They were ascending the shallow steps to the palace, which Celie noticed with fascination were set with seashells, when Rufus came screeching down from the sky to land on the top step in front of them.

Celie braced herself, figuring that Queen Amatopeia was probably going to scream. Most ladies did when they saw a griffin for the first time, and Lulath's mother was a very vocal person to begin with.

But she'd forgotten about the queen's competent dog handling. This was a woman who knew animals, and loved them. And so, too, did the king.

The royal couple instantly went still, which was the best thing they could have done. Then, in a reverent and hushed voice, the queen asked if she could approach the griffin.

"What whom does he seek?" the king asked, also in a very quiet voice.

"It's, er, Rufus," Celie said. "He's mine. I suppose he's seeking me."

She stepped forward and grabbed hold of Rufus's harness. She gave him a little shake and then stroked his head. He cooed and butted her in the chest.

"What are you doing, bad boy!" Celie scolded. "You're supposed to stay with Pogue and the ship!"

Pogue Parry, a knight and a good friend of all the Glower family, was coming after them with the parts of a massive ship that was Lilah and Lulath's wedding gift from Celie's father, King Glower. He was also bringing a wagon containing toys, harnesses, and food for the various griffins, as well as Rolf's newly hatched Dagger-the-Golden, who was too small to fly for long.

Queen Amatopeia had sidled closer, and now she slowly extended her hand. She raised her eyebrows at Celie and waited for Celie's nod before moving her hand closer to Rufus. Rufus sniffed her hand delicately, and then he lashed his long lion tail and squawked.

"He likes you," Celie translated.

"Here comes my Lady," Queen Celina said, pointing to the sky. "She's the queen of the griffins," she explained to the Grathians. "And we call her Lady Griffin."

"Wondrous," whispered King Kurlath.

The lithe golden figure circled above them twice before she landed beside her son, Rufus. The queen of the griffins had attached herself to Queen Celina after they had brought her from the griffins' home world of Hatheland, where the Castle had also been built, centuries before. Lord Griffin—her mate and the king of the griffins—was bonded to King Glower, but even more so to the Castle, and so he had stayed home with the king to watch over the Castle and Sleyne. Queen Celina stroked Lady Griffin's head, and then invited King Kurlath to be sniffed and approved by the griffin queen.

Lilah's Juliet and Lulath's Lorcan the Destroyer were not far behind. Rolf scanned the skies for his griffin, but Dagger had only just started to fly while they were on their journey and wouldn't have been able to keep up.

Celie knew that Pogue wouldn't have let a griffin as young as Dagger take off on his own anyway. The carts with the ship and the griffins were almost a day behind them at this point, since they had rushed ahead in the royal carriage to meet Lulath's family. Only a strong flier with a good sense of direction could have followed them.

"Oh, they are the darlings!" Queen Amatopeia enthused. "But Lulath! Lorcan the Destroyer? What a name for this fine beast!"

"I am being this fond of our ancestor Lorcan," Lulath said stiffly.

His mother just shook her head and shared a look with Lilah. "And this is being your darling?" she asked Lilah, holding out a gentle hand to Juliet.

Lilah proudly introduced Juliet. Even Celie had to admit that Juliet was a beautiful griffin: delicately boned, sleek, her fur and feathers a shining bright gold with a hint of cream at the tips of her wings. Rufus was more stocky in build, larger, and a darker gold, with copper-brown markings on his wings. Celie thought him to be the finest of all griffins, of course, but Juliet looked like an artist's ideal of the animal.

The doors to the palace opened again, and a small gray-and-white dog sidled out. It took one look at the griffins and its puffy tail drooped. Rufus, meanwhile, saw it and hissed.

"No!" Celie grabbed Rufus's harness. "Don't you dare!"

"Oh, the horror!" King Kurlath said, throwing up his hands. "Will they be having the small dogs for eating?"

"No, because they know better," Celie said, making her voice stern and looking at Rufus as she said it.

"They want to play with the dogs," Lilah said, pulling back on Juliet's harness. "But the way they play is too rough. They tear their toys apart when they play."

"Oh, very," Queen Amatopeia said, and apparently could think of nothing to add. Celie didn't blame her. The entire palace was full of griffin chew toys.

"We can be taking the griffins to the gardens direct," King Kurlath said. "And then we must be thinking careful of the dogs and the birds and where they are being."

Lulath's mother let out a small scream. "And where are being your only darlings, my son?" she demanded. "Where are being JouJou and Kitsi, Bisi, and Niro?"

"They are in the carriage," Lilah was quick to assure her. "In their travel baskets. One of the servants is bringing them."

"Are you thinking I would be giving up my darling girls? Even for so fine of a griffin?" Lulath looked mortally offended.

"It is being only a question," his mother said, mollified. "Now, to be following this way, please!"

She led them away from the front doors and across the side of the courtyard to a high, arched doorway in a wall inlaid with beautiful pale-pink seashells. Celie made herself a promise to explore every inch of the Grathian royal palace and touch the beautiful shells that decorated it.

But for now she led Rufus through the arched doorway and into a long tunnel formed by an arching row of trees with purple flowers that dangled like grapes. She did reach out and touch the flowers, and Rufus snatched a bunch and then spit them out. Celie would have been embarrassed, but King Kurlath saw and laughed.

"They are the precious, are they not?"

Celie felt a wave of relief wash over her. She loved Lulath, and would never be embarrassed by anything she said or did in front of him—or anything Rufus did, either—but she had worried the whole way to Grath that perhaps Lulath's parents were different. Perhaps they were very formal or very stiff in their manners, the way Lulath had first appeared to be, with his fancy clothes and fastidious habits. She had often wondered if Lulath's stories about his family's many pets were true (although now they knew for certain that he was not exaggerating when he talked about the dogs), or if he had been sent to stay in Sleyne because his family wanted to be rid of him.

Judging from the warm welcome they had all received, his parents hadn't sent him to Sleyne to be rid of him. And they really did seem eager to add Lilah to their family as well. And of course they liked dogs; Celie herself was very fond of dogs, and Lulath's girls in particular.

But griffins were another matter—though it did look as if Lulath's parents were prepared to welcome griffins into their home.

"Ah! This very garden!" King Kurlath said, throwing open another arched door. "Please to be thinking of it always and forever as your garden, our family of the Glower!" He swept forward and then turned to beckon to them with both hands.

The griffins didn't need any encouragement. They jostled and squawked as they left their people behind and tried to be the first through the door. Finally the tangle of wings and talons was clear and the two-legged creatures could follow them. Celie let her mother and the Grathian queen go first, then Lilah and Lulath and Rolf, so she was last and couldn't see anything for a moment, just griffins and the backs of her family and friends, who had all gone silent.

Celie didn't know what had happened, at first. But then everyone began to wander slowly forward, and she was able to get a look at this very garden, which had just been presented to them.

It was breathtaking.

Banks of exotic flowers filled the garden with color and perfume. The close-cropped lawn was the color of emeralds, and here and there were stone benches or tables that were inlaid with shells the creamy white of the finest pearls. Across the garden was a low stone wall, and Rufus rambled over to it with Celie at his heels. When they got there, Celie gasped at what she saw.

Beyond the wall the ground dropped away, and hundreds of paces below them was something Celie had never seen before.

The sea.

Chapter
2

⊂≶⊃

The Royal Palace of Grath, the official name of which translated into Sanctuary by the Sea, was distractingly lovely. Every line of the Sanctuary seemed to have been drawn by an artist's hand, and every stone placed with an artist's eye. Where Celie's beloved Castle Glower was pleasantly sturdy and functional, the Sanctuary was made entirely for beauty. This meant that not every room was comfortable, and some bits of the Sanctuary had silk ropes draped across them, because they were too fragile to be used. But it was all very fascinating, and took Celie's mind off other things. Most of the time.

"I don't like it here," Celie announced on the fifth day.

They were out in their garden, overlooking the sea, eating breakfast. They ate breakfast and lunch there every day, and Celie spent a great deal of time watching the ocean and trying to keep Rufus from plunging headfirst over the wall. She had no objection to him flying over the water, and she had twice ridden him herself as he dipped his toes in the waves, but he had a fascination with the cliff that worried her. It would be like him to test his speed by diving off and seeing how close to the rocks at the bottom he could get before extending his wings.

"What do you mean? It's so beautiful," Lilah said.

She was reclining on a bench, sunning herself. Juliet lay on the grass beside her, also basking. Lilah was beautifully attired in pink silk trimmed with blond lace, which had been yet another gift from Queen Amatopeia. The queen seemed to think of Lilah as a sort of large doll to dress and coo over, and Lilah loved every minute of it. Celie thought it was quite disgusting.

"I. Don't. Like. It. Here," Celie repeated.

"Celie, why do you have to be this way?" Lilah closed her eyes and groaned. "You're going to be awful the entire time, aren't you?"

"Yes, Celie, what is wrong?" Queen Celina said, looking up from her knitting.

Far from her usual unruffled self, the queen looked peevish, and Celie could tell from her mother's voice that if she didn't choose her next words carefully, she would be in trouble.

"The Sanctuary is beautiful," Celie said honestly. "And the king and queen are the nicest people I have ever met."

"Then why don't you like it?" Lilah said impatiently.

"It's . . . There's just . . ."

"If your bed isn't comfortable, tell a servant. If your new gowns are uncomfortable, tell the seamstress," Queen Celina said. Then she swore.

Her daughters looked at her in shock.

"Sorry," she said, her smooth cheeks turning red. "I dropped a stitch. I know that's no excuse, but . . ."

"I'm not the only one who doesn't like it here," Celie said, pointing an accusing finger at her mother.

"I'm sorry, I'm sorry," Queen Celina said, giving up on picking up the stitch and tossing her knitting aside.

The ball of yarn unspooled and rolled across the lawn until it ran up against Lady Griffin's hip. The queen of the griffins looked up at the queen of Sleyne, then down at the ball of yarn, and made a noise of disgust. She scooted a few inches to the side so that the yarn wasn't touching her anymore, and then went back to sleep.

"You don't like it here?" Lilah sat up slowly, her fists clenching in the trailing sleeves of her gown. She opened and closed her mouth twice. "But Mother, *why?*" she asked, her voice plaintive.

"I don't know, dear, it's just . . . well, it's always hard to be away from home."

"The Sanctuary isn't alive," Rolf said, coming across the garden to them.

He had been down at the docks with Pogue and Master Cathan, the shipwright, all morning. He was wearing a lightweight sailor's tunic and loose trousers, and was brown from the sun, after having worked on the ship back in Sleyne throughout the spring as well. He looked almost grown up, and very strange for a moment. Celie didn't like that, either.

"This is the longest any of us has gone sleeping outside the Castle," Rolf said, kicking at the base of a birdbath.

The bowl of the bath was made of a giant clamshell, and Celie had already asked twice if it was a fake. It wasn't, apparently, and she hoped to never see a live clam that big. It could probably bite off her entire arm.

"It's the longest we've eaten outside the Castle, slept, spoke, worked," Rolf continued. "Even when we went to Hatheland, we were there only a few days."

"Your father and Bran and I were living outside the Castle for months last year," the queen pointed out. "And that was dreadful; but we were also injured."

Rolf nodded, looking grim.

Last year all of Sleyne had thought that the king and queen and Bran, Celie's oldest brother, were dead, after an evil foreign prince had paid bandits to kill them. They had gone into hiding in the forest until they were well enough to travel home to the Castle.

"But as you say," Rolf went on, "you were hurt. You already didn't feel well, and you had bigger problems to worry you." He hunched his shoulders, settling the loose linen tunic. "This is the longest any of us have been outside the Castle by choice."

"Except for Bran, again, when he went to the College of Wizardry," Lilah pointed out.

"But *Bran* isn't here," Rolf said in exasperation. "I'm not talking about *Bran*! I'm talking about *us*! Why we feel out of sorts!"

"What are we supposed to do?" Lilah wailed. "We're supposed to be here for months! And I feel all . . . *floppy*!"

Rolf turned his head. "So, I was right," he called out.

"Are they coming?" Pogue called back.

He was in the gateway of the garden. He, too, wore a loose tunic, and high boots with his linen trousers. There was a red cloth tying his shoulder-length hair back, and he was even more tanned than Rolf. Celie felt even stranger, and not just because of the Sanctuary. Pogue Parry was widely considered to be the most handsome young man in Castle Glower or the village, but it appeared that he was even considered handsome in the sophisticated Grathian court.

"They're coming," Rolf said.

"Where?" Celie demanded, trying to cover up her fluster of feelings.

"To see the ship, and touch it," Rolf said. "It's part of the Castle; it will do you good!"

So they made their way down to the private docks that belonged to the royal family. In Sleyne, they simply would have walked out through the Castle gates and down the road, but in Grath things were always more complicated. First they had to find their hosts and tell them where they wanted to go, and the king and queen had to finish feeding their exotic birds, which lived in a glass-roofed room filled with tropical plants. Then they had to order a parade of coaches to take the Glower family to the docks, and while the coaches were being made ready, they had to change into suitable ship-viewing clothes.

This last was at Lilah's insistence, not so much a rule of the Grathian court. But Celie wasn't imagining the approval on Queen Amatopeia's face when they told her good-bye in the courtyard. She was a deeply kind woman, but she also changed her clothes at least four times a day, and Celie knew that the queen found Celie's habit of wearing the same gown all day distressing.

Celie wanted Queen Amatopeia to like her, because she loved Lulath like a brother and she knew it was important to Lilah that they impress her future mother-in-law. But when you spent at least part of your day rolling around in the grass with a griffin, it was hard to see the point in changing one mostly clean gown for another, just because the clock struck a certain hour.

It was hard to remember, too, that even the dinners with just Lulath's parents and one or two of his siblings counted as official state dinners, and not family dinners. In the Castle, state dinners were rare, and though Glower family dinners included Lulath, Pogue, and often several members of the Royal Council, King Glower himself often sat down with his collar askew and ink splotches on his sleeves.

It was nearly an hour before they were rolling down the smooth-paved roads of Taran, the seaside capital of

Grath. The Sanctuary sat on the southern cliff that overlooked the sea, and Taran was laid out on the sloping hill to the north and west, extending to the grasslands north of the ocean and the low docks on the west.

The buildings were higher and the streets wider than in Sleyne City, but the people seemed no less friendly. They stopped and waved to the royal coaches as Celie and her family passed through the streets. Children shouted out, asking where the griffins were, and Celie waved and pointed upward. Far above them the griffins circled, and the children screamed in delight when they spotted them.

The road along the docks curled to follow the line of the shore, with the city on the right side of the coaches and the long wooden docks full of ships on their left. Celie climbed over Lilah and stuck her head out the window to look at all the ships. Some were narrow and sleek with blue sails, while others had yellow sails and little hatches close to the waterline, where oars would be put out and the ship could be rowed in calm winds.

They passed ships from every country, except for landlocked Sleyne, and then they came to a long beach, where no docks were built but a rocky construct jutted out into the water. Rolf called something back from the coach in front of them, but Celie couldn't understand.

"Those are the ruins of the old palace," Lilah said. "Apparently the first palace of Grath was built right on the water, but a huge storm destroyed most of it."

"Oh," Celie said.

She couldn't blame them for wanting to build the new palace so high on the cliff, then, if all that was left of the previous palace was part of a wall. If Lilah hadn't said something, she would have just assumed it was a pile of rocks that happened to be there, not the ruins of an entire palace.

Then they were passing docks again, but these were patrolled by soldiers in the blue uniforms of the Grathian Guard. The buildings on the right side of the coaches were all official looking, and the ships on the left were all of the same design: sleek and tall, with blue sails and the names of Grathian kings painted in gold on the bows.

At the end of the row of Grathian ships was a great deal of lumber and a great many men shouting and swearing and swinging things around with ropes and pulleys. Off to one side were the huge carts that had been used to haul the parts of the ship from Sleyne.

Perched atop the nearest cart was Bright Arrow, Pogue's griffin. When he had realized that they were going to change their clothes and ride in carriages, Pogue had left for the docks on his own. Now he climbed down from a wooden support frame and bowed to Queen Celina.

She smiled fondly back. "How is the building going, Sir Pogue?" she asked.

"Well enough," he said. "As far as I can tell."

"Is there something wrong?" Lilah asked anxiously. She looked at the ship, and then back at Pogue. "I mean,

I know you're working very hard, but you've never built a ship before . . ."

"Lilah," their mother said in a warning tone.

"Is that what this is?" Pogue asked. "You're checking to make certain I don't ruin your ship?"

"Where is Master Cathan?" Lilah demanded. "I thought you were just here to help the shipwright, not actually build the ship."

"Is this what happens when we leave the Castle?" Celie asked Rufus, who had landed beside her. "We just bicker and act awful and feel awful?"

Her own unease—that feeling she had had at the Sanctuary that she didn't belong and needed to go—was actually worse now. She felt even more strange and feverish, and she could tell by the way Pogue and Lilah were arguing that they felt it, too. Arrow, from his perch on the cart, began to shriek in distress, and Juliet wouldn't land at all; she just circled above them in agitation.

"What is that?" Celie said to Rufus. He cocked his head to one side, and she could see that his attention was on it as well.

There was an enormous wooden frame all around where the ship was being built. Inside the frame, the ship was already a sort of wooden skeleton, much farther along than Celie would have thought it could be in a week. To one side were enormous timbers, smoothed and planed and carefully stacked, ready to make up the sides and decks. One of the carts still held large crates of sails, carefully packed instruments, and the canvas-wrapped figurehead that had started all of this.

Celie had found the figurehead, a beautifully carved and gilded griffin, in a storage room in the Castle, along with the original sails and many of the parts of the Builder's Ship. The Builder of the Castle—the ancient king who had ruled a country called Hatheland and fought alongside griffins and created the Castle that Celie loved—had also been known for his ship, which was being re-created now for Lilah and Lulath.

Sleyne was nowhere near the ocean and didn't have a lake large enough to sail such a ship on. Celie had to grudgingly admit that it would be better to give the new ship to her sister and Lulath than to keep the figurehead propped up in the corner of the throne room.

But during the last few months, as Celie and her family had chased an evil wizard through passages inside the very walls of the Castle, Celie had found that parts of the Castle had been created not by the Builder but by his enemies from the Glorious Arkower. Rather than destroying these things, Celie had hit upon the idea of using them—of creating a ship that would have parts from Sleyne, Hatheland, Grath, and the Glorious Arkower.

Which, Celie saw, was the current problem.

The figurehead would be the very last thing to be put on the ship, except for the sails. Even Celie, with no experience in building ships, could see that. So she could understand why those things were off to one side. But what she and Rufus had seen was a big pile of doors, doors that had once concealed the secret passages the Arkish had built. They weren't stacked neatly, the way the other materials were. They were tossed aside, and men were walking over them, looking irritated, as they went about their jobs.

"Pogue," Celie said.

But Pogue and Lilah were now in a heated argument, and Queen Celina was doing nothing to stop them. Arrow had flown up to join Juliet and Lady Griffin, but they weren't playing, they were circling around and around in agitation, screeching at each other. It was making the workmen nervous, and Celie didn't blame them. Even if you didn't know anything about griffins, there was no mistaking the sound of an animal that was growing angry.

"Pogue!" Celie said again, louder and more insistently.

"What? What do you want?" he snapped.

Celie recoiled as though he'd struck her. Pogue had never spoken to her so harshly before. She grabbed Rufus's harness too tight, and he protested.

"How dare you use that tone with my sister!" Lilah raged.

Celie was more hurt than offended, and also more suspicious than ever that something was terribly wrong. Instead of joining in the fight or reprimanding Pogue, she chose to ignore it and just pointed to the haphazard stack of doors.

"Why aren't they taking better care of those?" Celie asked, though she already knew the answer.

"They decided not to use them," he said curtly, and turned back to Lilah.

"No, that's wrong," Celie said.

No one was listening to her. Lilah and Pogue were right back into their fight, and Queen Celina was fanning the flames by insisting that they talk to the Grathian shipwright, Master Cathan. Rolf was simply staring into space, muttering something, but Celie decided that he was her best bet anyway, and went over to tug at his sleeve. She had to yank on his arm to get him to look at her.

"Rolf!"

"I thought it would make us feel better," Rolf was muttering. "But it feels worse."

"Yes, it feels worse," she said, shaking his arm again. "Because they're doing it wrong!"

"What?" Rolf looked at her, and then back at the ship. "How can you tell? You don't know how to build a ship. And they do."

"*The ship doesn't like it,*" Celie insisted. "Can't you feel it? It's making us feel wrong because *it* feels wrong. The Castle wants the ship to be made with parts from all the different lands, and they're not doing it!"

She yanked his arm yet again and pointed at the discarded pile of doors with her free hand. Just as she did, one of the men tromped across a door in his heavy work boots, and there was a distinct cracking noise.

The sound woke Rolf up. He shook himself, dislodging Celie's hand, and started toward the men, calling out. Celie followed him, pulling on Rufus's harness to keep her griffin from diving at the workers. If she needed any proof that this was the problem, Rufus's behavior convinced her. None of the griffins had liked the Arkish tunnels hidden in the Castle, but even Rufus seemed to take the mistreatment of the Arkish doors as a personal insult.

"Rufus, stop; we'll fix it," she said, gritting her teeth and tugging to keep him from snapping his beak at one of the workmen.

"My only good sir," Rolf called in Grathian to the man who had just cracked one of the doors. "May I be having a speaking to you if it pleases the queen?"

Celie winced. Between her tutor, Master Humphries, and Lulath, they had gotten a comprehensive education in the Grathian language and culture, but Rolf had never been a very diligent student. Celie wondered if she should take over, but the man seemed to be able to follow her brother's convoluted grammar.

"These are being doors for the untimely use of the ship," Rolf said heatedly. "And now to have ripped it!"

The man glanced around, startled. He was holding a keg full of long iron nails, and now he handed them off to another man and came forward, wiping his hands on the seat of his pants.

"I'm very sorry, Your Highness," the man said.

Celie did her best not to wince at how much more refined this shipyard worker sounded than her brother.

"But Master Cathan has decided that we aren't going to use these doors," the man went on. "If you would like them for another project, we will have them packed up and sent to the Sanctuary."

"It is not being the Sanctuary of needing doors!" Rolf insisted.

"Pardon me, but where *is* Master Cathan?" Celie asked in her much more polished Grathian. "We should speak to him about this."

The man looked only too glad to pass them off to the master shipbuilder. By now they had attracted the attention of many of the workers, as well as Lilah, Pogue, and their mother, who had stopped arguing to come and see what was wrong.

"It's the doors," Celie said to her mother. "The Castle—the ship, I suppose—wants them. That's why we feel awful."

Her mother just looked at her, uncomprehending.

Rolf squatted down and began to look at the crack in the door. "I think this can be fixed," he said.

Celie hummed her approval. She was watching the workman talking to Master Cathan, who had slithered down a rope from higher up in the framing around the ship. She could tell by his expression, even from this distance, that he was not pleased to see them. But when he reached them he bowed and greeted them with his usual courtesy.

"Master Cathan," Celie said. "I thought we had agreed these doors would be used on the ship."

"Ah, indeed we did, Your Highness," he said. If he was surprised that she was speaking Grathian, he didn't show it, but just answered in the same language. "Now that we are here in Grath, with so many fine materials available to us, it seems a shame to use these old, less reliable things." He scuffed a foot at the doors.

"Have a stop to that," Rolf said sharply.

"*That's* why you don't want to use them?" Pogue said in Sleynth, sounding dazed. "Because they're *old?*"

"And Grathian wood—" the shipbuilder began.

"Grathian wood is being of fine," Lilah interrupted, folding her arms. "But the point of ship of mine is to use the woods and . . . and things not of wood . . . from *all* the place. Sleyne. Grath. Hatheland. Glorious Arkower, who is are our enemies."

"I know your vision for the ship was very fine," Cathan said with a simper. "But I must say, as a shipbuilder, well, I know you want your ship to be . . . the best."

"Why is not an Arkish doors make not the best?" Lilah demanded. "The wood is finest quality, and thus finely carved!"

27

"It's not something you can understand, Your Highness," Cathan began.

"You have lies," Queen Celina said. Then she switched to Sleynth, so that she would sound more regal, Celie guessed. "My oldest daughter is correct: there is no reason these doors cannot be used. Why don't you want to honor our wishes?"

Master Cathan looked at all of them and swallowed visibly. "Well, because—" he began in Sleynth. "I am not knowing of what importance? I am thinking that the small princess is of frugal mind being?" He nodded at Celie.

"Well, I wasn't," Celie said, feeling her cheeks burn.

"We have plenty of money," Lilah said at the same time, blushing in anger rather than embarrassment. "However, we are trying to unify several countries with the ship, something we thought you understood."

Master Cathan frowned. He looked into the distance, trying to look noble and thoughtful, but Celie could tell it was an act. He'd stayed in Castle Glower for several months, getting the ship ready for the journey to Grath. He had agreed with their plans then, even if he was—

"You're afraid?" Celie blurted out. "What are you afraid of?"

"I am not having fear," Cathan said weakly. "I am having . . . easier to make doors to the ship, not making ship to the doors."

Rolf shook his head and tutted, and Lilah rolled her eyes. Pogue frowned, and Celie felt rather bad for him. He'd enjoyed learning from Master Cathan, she knew, and now he was probably wondering if the man had lied about other things.

"I might be able to help with that," Queen Celina said, thoughtful. Her fingers danced in the air, almost as if she were knitting. "Stretching or shrinking the doors a bit wouldn't be too difficult."

"No!" Master Cathan shouted, his face shiny with sweat. "No magic!"

"Oh," Celie said. *"That's* what you're afraid of."

Chapter
3

Celie perched on a stack of Grathian lumber beside
the figurehead. Rufus lounged beside her, looking casual,
but Celie knew he was watching, too. And what they
were watching was not unlike an elaborate play. Queen
Celina and Master Cathan were facing each other across
a stack of wooden doors, while Rolf and Pogue stood to
one side in silence, and Lilah stood on the other side and
translated.

Fortunately, Celie's Grathian was very good, and the
pile of lumber and the figurehead were close enough that
she could listen in. She draped an arm around the figurehead's neck, which wasn't very comfortable, but one of
the workmen saw her and gave her an admiring look, so
she kept her arm there and tried to look comfortable and
royal at the same time, which was no mean feat.

What she heard soon distracted her from the growing numbness in her arm and made both her and Rufus more and more angry. Celie was angry because of the words coming out of Master Cathan's mouth, but Rufus was just angry because Celie was. Either way, they both finally sat bolt upright on the edge of the stack of lumber, Rufus hissing and Celie glaring.

It seemed that although Master Cathan had treated Pogue with great respect in Sleyne, once he returned to his own land he had demanded to be put in charge of the ship. This seemed to have come after the realization, during the journey, that while Pogue was a knight, he had been born the son of a blacksmith. Master Cathan was of noble family, and was not going to take orders from a commoner.

"Oh, yes, you will," Queen Celina said through Lilah. She repeated herself in accented Grathian.

Celie was shocked that someone could be so awful, just because they were taking orders from a commoner. And what orders? Master Cathan was the shipbuilder. Pogue was just there to make sure the proper materials were used. And the orders to use the doors and other parts from the Castle had come from King Glower, Celie's father. Just because Pogue was the one carrying out the orders didn't make them any less important!

It seemed that it did. Because of the magic. Master Cathan had not liked being in the Castle. It had made

31

him nervous, but Celie hadn't known he truly feared and despised magic. Now that King Glower wasn't there to give him orders directly, he had decided that Pogue was too foolishly common to know that magic was dangerous, and any parts that had touched magic should not be included on a ship.

Now Celie and Rufus were both hissing.

"I want you gone," Lilah said.

"Lilah," Queen Celina said, turning to Lilah in surprise.

"If you work not with and beside magic, then you work not on this my ship," Lilah said in Grathian, and then she repeated herself to their mother in Sleynth.

Celie expected their mother to scold Lilah, to tell her to stop being so spoiled. But instead Queen Celina frowned at Master Cathan for a long time. Now he was sweating again, but this time not from the threat of magic.

In a very careful voice, translated as precisely as possible by Lilah, Queen Celina informed Master Cathan that Sir Pogue was a most trusted friend of the royal family of Sleyne, and that his word was to be considered the word of the Glower family. She explained that the ship was a part of Castle Glower, and as such needed to have the magic of the Castle in it. It also, she said with great disdain, needed to have every piece of it treated with respect.

At this she turned and looked directly at one of the men who had been walking over the discarded doors. He turned red and began to stack them more neatly.

"Are you willing to do as we ask?" Queen Celina finished.

Master Cathan looked caught. He glanced around and saw Celie sitting with her arm around the figurehead, her angry griffin by her side. He threw his hands in the air.

"No," he said in Sleynth. "I am not being this man of which you seek. I am not being a man who greets the griffins and the magic."

And then he marched off.

Most of the men had stopped working, listening to their master and the queen. About a dozen of them also left, following at Master Cathan's heels. Rolf gave them a disgusted look, and so did Celie, but Pogue just looked stoic.

Celie wondered, for the first time, if it was hard for him to be a knight. She'd thought he would love it, since he hadn't wanted to be a blacksmith but had dreamed of living and working in the Castle with the Glower family. But outside the Castle, was it difficult for him? Away from friends and family who were proud of him, did people think he didn't deserve to be a knight?

He caught her eye and gave her a grim little smile.

"Who's going to build the ship now?" Rolf demanded. "What do we do?"

"Pogue?" Celie called from her perch. "Do you know how to finish the ship?"

Pogue shook his head. A few more of the men put

down their tools, made guilty little bows to the royal family, and then slunk away.

"It seems I am be coming just at the right!" called a merry voice.

A bowlegged, barrel-chested man was striding along the docks, dressed so marvelously that at first Celie didn't notice what was on his shoulder. He was wearing elaborate layers of tucked and frilled clothing, like any noble Grathian, but his were made entirely of brown leather. Celie had never seen a ruffled collar made of leather before, but when she took her eyes off it to look at the man's face, she screamed.

On his shoulder there was a strange creature that resembled a person! It was completely covered in gray hair, with a wizened, elderly face, although it was as small as a baby. Celie stared in horror.

The leather-clad man saw her looking, and laughed.

"Having never seen such a monk as this, I am thinking of you," he said to Celie. He stretched out his arm, and the little creature ran down it, displaying a long tail.

"What is that?" Lilah shrieked.

The man laughed. "It is being only a monk! Of the greenest vining jungles!"

"What does it do?" Celie asked, intrigued. Rufus looked like he was ready to fly or bite, so she stayed where she was with a firm hand on his harness.

"It is being a precious awful pet," the man said with a shrug. "An only way to say to my family that they are having many of the dogs, and many of the goats, and many of the birds, and many of the ponies, but I am he who is having the only monk!"

"Wait," Lilah said. "Are you—"

"That is right, my our Delilah," he said with a laugh that boomed out across the shipyard. "I am being your very new soon brother, Orlath! Prince Orlath! Explorer of jungles! Captain of ships! And builder of many the fine!" Orlath tossed the monk toward his shoulder, where it grabbed hold, and then he put his fists on his hips. "I am the one coming here and the now to make this ship be built!"

"I was not expecting that," Rolf said faintly.

"None of us were," Queen Celina said, but then she smiled.

Chapter
4

⟨≈⟩

Master Cathan had been right: the ship was magic. But it was the kind of magic that Celie and her family were familiar with, the magic of Castle Glower. The ship truly was a part of the Castle, as they had hoped, and it had let them know that it wasn't happy. Unlike the Castle, it didn't seem to be able to grow a new room or make itself bigger or smaller, but apparently what it could do was make the entire Glower family testy and prone to fighting.

"But now I feel like a new man," Rolf marveled again, nearly a week later, picking up a basket of nails and staggering toward the ship.

"One day you will be the new man," Orlath said. "But today you are still I think the old boy." He laughed and took the heavy basket from Rolf and hooked it to a rope for one of the men to haul up the side of the half-built ship.

Rolf blushed and muttered something, and Celie and Pogue exchanged grins when he wasn't looking. But Orlath just clapped him on the shoulder and laughed again.

"It is good, to be being feeling so better," he said. "It is good to be doing of a thing that someone is having in love."

"What?"

"It's good to have a passion in life," Orlath said in Grathian. "Like myself and ships, or Lulath with his wars."

"That's still being much weird me," Rolf said in Grathian. "Lulath being this battle expert." He shook his head in bemusement.

"Why else would he name his griffin Lorcan the Destroyer?" Orlath said, shaking his own head.

"Who *was* Lorcan the Destroyer?" Celie asked with a grunt. She was sitting in her usual spot atop a pile of lumber under the watchful eye of the figurehead and trying to master a series of knots that Orlath had showed her with a piece of rope.

"My brother will having the telling to you," Orlath said. "I would rather be talking of the ship and the sea!" He made a sweeping gesture, a smile splitting his face from ear to ear.

"I don't know that I have a passion for all ships," Rolf said, getting back to their earlier conversation. "I'm mainly interested in this one."

"Ah, but that is what I meant," Orlath explained, switching to Grathian. "Your passion, your life, it revolves around your beloved Castle Glower. You are the keepers of the Castle, the scholars of its history, and when you are far from it, you are unhappy. And when the ship, made from its very bones, is displeased, then you are the only ones who can guess this!"

"I am supposing this we are," Rolf said, looking pleased. "Aren't we so, Cel?"

"Mm-hmm," she said, still trying to get the knot right. She pulled one of the ends, and the whole thing fell apart. "Drat!"

"Like this," Pogue said, setting down the long curved piece of wood he had braced on his shoulder. He took the rope from her and held it up. "Over, under, around, and through, that's the way we like to do," he chanted, and then showed her the finished knot.

"Did you really just say that?" Rolf said, and burst out laughing.

Pogue turned red under his tan. But Celie took the rope, studied the knot, and then managed to do it herself, saying the rhyme under her breath. She mutely held it up to show Rolf, and to make him stop laughing. He clapped when he saw, but he was still laughing.

"Of a sureness I should be knowing that Sir Pogue would have the gift of it," Orlath said with enthusiasm.

Yet another nice change was that Prince Orlath thought Pogue was astonishing. He had sung his praises to the skies upon hearing that this noble knight, trainer of griffins, builder of ships, had been born in a blacksmith's cottage. He had been quick to share stories of sea captains he had known, and heroes of Grathian legend, who had risen from humble beginnings to greatness.

Orlath listened to everything Pogue said, and carefully considered each piece of the ship they had brought from Sleyne, making it clear that he wanted to use everything they had. He wanted to know the history of the Castle, of Hatheland and the Glorious Arkower, and it was Pogue he wanted to hear it from. Celie and Rolf translated, but Pogue was picking up Grathian very quickly. He had already begun learning the important ship-related words from the Grathian workmen, and Orlath wasn't the only one impressed by how quickly Pogue was soaking up words and whole phrases.

"Now, Celie, once you figure out the knots, we will teach you the lines and rigging, and what the various sails are for," Orlath said in Grathian. He had also expressed great delight and admiration for Celie's mastery of his language, and usually addressed her directly in it. "But that will have to wait until there are sails in place!"

"Maybe I could learn to use a hammer?" Celie asked eagerly. "I would really like to hammer some of the parts of the ship!"

"That would to me be the alarming," Rolf remarked.

"I am sure nothing would please the ship more than to have all the family help," Orlath said. "We shall teach them many things about building a fine ship, Sir Pogue!"

"But not now," Celie said with a sigh.

She pointed up the road from the Sanctuary. A royal coach was coming toward them. A footman leaped down from his perch on the back of the coach as soon as it stopped, but the door burst open before he could reach it. Out poured four familiar small dogs—Lulath's own dogs—followed by their master and Lilah.

"What joys, friends!" Lulath exclaimed. "What growth of the ship!"

His mouth was smiling, but Celie could see that there was no smile in his eyes, and Lilah looked like a thundercloud. The dogs milled around, yapping and causing problems, until Rufus led them over to a pile of lumber to play hide-and-go-seek, and then the people were free to talk.

"Are you being coming to look at this, the growth of your ship?" Orlath said. "Will this my fair sister see her gift?" He held out an arm to lead Lilah toward the ship for a tour, but she shook her head.

"I'm sorry," she said. "I know you're all working hard, but really we came to—well, I wanted to ask Rolf and Celie to—"

"To be speaking of the sense into my brain," Lulath said, cheerfully enough. But Celie still thought his eyes looked shadowed.

"What is it?" Pogue asked. "What's happened?"

"It is being no large thing," Lulath said.

"It is!" Lilah protested. "It is being—I mean, it is a very large thing!"

"Just stop being coy and tell us what it is, then," Rolf said in frustration.

The frustration was partly because Dagger had tried to hide with Nisi in the lumber and gotten stuck. Celie helped pull the small griffin out, while Lilah collapsed atop a barrel of nails.

"Lulath is going to lead an envoy to the village by the sea," Lilah said, her tone heavy with meaning.

Celie and Rolf looked at each other, faces blank. They were standing right by the sea themselves. Most villages in Grath were by the sea.

"*The* village by the sea," Lilah said with even greater emphasis.

Celie was still confused. It didn't help when Lilah pointed up the shore, to the east. It really didn't help when Lulath gently took her arm and moved it so that she was pointing more toward the south.

"What are you talking about?" Rolf asked.

"The griffin rider village," Lilah said at last. "You know? Lulath is going there tomorrow. *Alone.*" She gave Lulath a dire look.

"You're going to the griffin rider village?" Celie's voice squeaked on the last word. "Can I come with you?"

"I want to go," Rolf declared.

"So do I!" Pogue added, while Orlath looked on in bemusement.

"And I want to go as well," Lilah said with asperity. "I

41

don't even care about the village itself! I don't want him to go alone! You have to help me talk sense into him!"

"I am not being alone," Lulath said, taking her hand and squeezing it. "I am being with the many guards, and the . . ." He frowned. "The . . . men who are taking the money for my king?"

"Tax collectors?" Celie supplied.

"Yes," Lulath said with a more genuine smile.

"Why now?" Celie asked curiously.

"An excellent question," Lilah agreed.

For many years there had been a village on the coast of Grath where the people spoke a language no one else could decipher, never allowed strangers within the village walls, and paid no taxes to the king of Grath. Lulath had once attempted to visit them, to try to learn their customs, but they would not allow even the jolly prince to enter.

Just recently, after returning from Hatheland and hearing the language spoken by Ethan, who had come to Sleyne to help care for the griffins, Lulath had realized where the people of this village were from. They were the last of the griffin riders, those who had followed the unicorns to the sea with the last of their griffins, and then stayed there as their griffins (and many of their own people, probably) had fallen ill from a plague called blackblister that they had brought with them from Hatheland.

They had all talked about going to the village to find out if their suspicions were correct when they got to

Grath. They thought that if these people were the old griffin riders, they would surely let the new griffin riders in the gates. But once they had gotten to the Sanctuary, in the excitement and stress of getting the ship built and meeting Lulath's family, they had not spoken of the closed village at all.

"But you're going now? Without us?" Celie asked.

"It is being better this way," Lulath pleaded. "My father is saying, if these are truly being those who did flee because of the blackblister, they are being cowards all, and he is wanting to speak to them. I am taking two tax men to say at last, will you pay some taxes to your king where you live now, and some of the soldiers, in case there is being a small fight. But my darlings are here in the safety." He held out his hands to encompass them all, even Rolf and Pogue.

This rather pleased Celie. Previously, only the dogs and Lorcan had been referred to as Lulath's darlings. It was nice to know that he loved them as much as his girls and his griffin. With anyone else, Celie would expect to be regarded as better than an animal, but Lulath had so much love for animals that it was really very flattering.

Rolf and Pogue looked as though they felt the same way. But Lilah? Not as much.

"You can't do this to me," she said to Lulath. "What if you die? And I'm left wondering what happened to you. Or how it happened to you."

"You . . . want to see him die?" Rolf asked, mystified.

"No," Lilah said impatiently. "I want him to live, which is why I don't want him out of my sight!"

They all just stared at her, except for Lulath, who sighed.

"My Lilah, my delight," he said, "I am sorry that you are having worry over this. But the king my father has commanded this so." He raised one hand to cut her off. "And it is not being because my father, he is having other sons and so is wanting to be rid of me," Lulath said.

Celie glared at her sister. Had Lilah really said such a thing? Lilah gave her a defiant look in return. It seemed that she had.

"It is being," Lulath went on, "because I am having the Ethan write down for me the common phrases of the tongue of his land, and I am being, with my many mistakes even so, a negotiator known of keenness," he said with dignity.

"You've been learning Arkish?" Celie said in amazement.

"Is there anything you don't know about?" Rolf said with a whistle. "The villagers are going to be dumbstruck!"

"I hate you all!" Lilah announced. Then she burst into tears and fled.

Chapter
5

~⚬~

The next day the entire court (and most of the palace animals) gathered to see Lulath and the tax collectors on their way to the griffin riders' village. The griffins had made an uneasy peace with the dogs, but everyone nevertheless kept their eyes open for any sign of a fight.

Celie had her hand firmly on Lorcan's harness, and Lilah stood on the other side of her betrothed's griffin, also keeping him in check. Her eyes were red, and she looked like she hadn't slept.

Which was not good, because Lorcan was becoming a problem.

The moment he'd seen Lulath step out in his riding clothes, he'd begun dancing around, clearly anticipating an outing. Though he couldn't yet carry Lulath long distances, he made it known (by hissing at Lulath's horse) that he wanted the prince to ride him on the first leg of the journey.

When Lulath had led him gently over to Lilah and Celie and told him to be the best griffin in the world and stay with the princesses, Lorcan had known immediately that he was being left behind, and he hadn't liked it one bit. Lulath had given him firm instructions, and Celie had put a hand on his harness, and he'd settled for a moment—but only a moment.

"My son, go forth and treat with these neighbors," King Kurlath was intoning in Grathian for the benefit of the court. "Learn the intent of their hearts, and ensure that we will continue together in peace."

"O my father, and my king," Lulath replied, "I do this gladly, and shall return soon with news, news that I pray will bring joy to all who hear it." He embraced the king, who kissed him on both cheeks.

Lorcan scraped his front talons across the white paving stones of the courtyard. Celie pressed down on his back, pinning him in place.

"Return to us safely and soon, my son," Queen Amatopeia said. She embraced Lulath and kissed his cheeks as well.

"Please my mother, look after my beautiful bride-to-be, who is more precious to me than my own life," Lulath said. It was the formal way of speaking, but Celie could hear the real emotion in Lulath's voice.

Lorcan lashed his tail and stretched his neck in a way that was all too casual.

"She is as my own daughter, and will be treasured near to my heart," Queen Amatopeia replied, as was expected. She reached across Juliet's back and took Lilah's hand, which wasn't part of the ritual, and Celie saw a single tear drip down Lilah's cheek.

Celie reached over Lorcan's back to touch Lilah's shoulder. Unfortunately, it gave Lorcan the chance he'd been waiting for.

He exploded out from between Celie and Lilah and burst right past Lulath. With one flap of his wings he soared to the top of the coach that would carry the two tax collectors and settled himself there, his talons digging into the wooden roof.

"Lorcan!" Lulath cried, waving his arms. "You come down here right now!"

"Lorcan, here, boy," Celie called. She pulled a pouch of dried figs from her sash and waved them at the griffin. "Your favorite! Come down!"

Now the other griffins began to squawk, wondering if they, too, needed to be upset. Lulath, Celie, and Lilah all gathered around the coach, trying to coax Lorcan down with promises of various treats—and the occasional threat of no treats if he didn't comply. Barking erupted from the coach, and Celie opened the door to see Lulath's dogs peeking out of their traveling baskets. Lulath had said that he would take them so that Lilah needn't worry about his griffin *and* his dogs, but Celie suspected that he just couldn't have parted with Lorcan and his girls all at once.

The four little dogs leaped down from the coach and turned to look up at the roof. Lorcan leaned his head over the edge and screeched at them. JouJou yapped fiercely, and Lorcan pulled back.

"I'll put them back in their baskets," Lilah said.

Just as she stooped to gather them up, Lorcan leaped down from the coach. Nisi barked now, and he cowered before the tiny, bow-bedecked creature. She strolled over and climbed up onto his back. The others followed, sitting on his legs and rump. Lorcan looked at Lulath and made a piteous noise.

"You'll have to leave the girls." Lilah sighed.

Celie set their travel baskets down by Lorcan. Then she picked up JouJou and stuck her under one arm so that she could take hold of Lorcan's harness with the other.

"It's going to be all right," she told Lulath.

He hugged Celie, then turned and tenderly kissed and hugged Lilah.

"It is best, Father, that I leave quickly, I think," he called in Grathian.

Lulath mounted his horse, and so did the soldiers who were guarding the party. The tax collectors hurried to get inside the coach. Celie supposed this arrangement was better for everyone: the girls would help keep Lorcan under control, and the tax collectors wouldn't have to share the coach with four dogs.

The court gave a cheer as the horses left the gates, and Celie and the Glower family joined in. As soon as the gates closed, Celie led Lorcan and the others to their garden. Lilah brought Juliet and Dagger, Pogue came with Arrow and Rufus, and soon Queen Celina and Lady Griffin joined them.

"Here we all are," Rolf said, rather glumly.

The dogs played on the grass, and Lorcan joined them. Celie stayed within reach, ready to leap at his harness if he showed signs of trying to follow Lulath now. Lady Griffin, who normally didn't pay attention to Lulath's girls, since she was not allowed to eat them, positioned herself nearby as well, and kept one eye on Lorcan in a motherly way.

"I think we'll be all right," Celie said. "We can do this."

"We don't have much of a choice," Lilah pointed out.

"The good news is, *I* don't have to sit here moping," Pogue said. "I've got to get back to the ship to help." Then he made a hasty bow toward Queen Celina. "If that is all right with Your Majesty?" he quickly asked.

"Yes, of course," she said, smiling. "You know how much we appreciate all the hard work you've done, Sir Pogue."

"Thank you, Your Majesty," Pogue said. He straightened and turned to Celie. "Do you want me to leave Arrow?"

"Please," Celie said. "I may need him to sit on Lorcan."

Bright Arrow was younger than Lorcan, but already bigger. In fact, he was nearly as big as Lord Griffin, and showed no signs of stopping soon. He ate twice as much as Rufus, and was muscular and sleek at the same time. He looked exactly like one of the fighting griffins depicted on the tapestries back in the Castle.

"If you children are engaged here," Queen Celina said, "I believe I'll go to my lesson with the Royal Wizard. He's teaching me all about poison," she said brightly.

"Mother!" Lilah said, shocked.

"And the antidotes," their mother said, waving her hand. "Don't fuss, Lilah."

Lady Griffin got up to follow Queen Celina out of the garden. As she passed, she carked some instruction to Lorcan, who ducked his head as though chastened.

"Stay here, Lady Griffin," Celie coaxed.

The griffin queen gave her a superior look, and Queen Celina looked over her shoulder. "No," she said. "Best to let her come with me. She's half wild herself."

They lined up the rest of the griffins, and Celie tried to teach them commands involving a short word and a hand gesture that would make the griffins pounce, or strike with a talon. It was actually quite fun, especially when they tied cushions to Rolf and got him to be the villain the griffins would attack. Lulath's girls watched from the safety of their baskets and swished their plumed tails and barked in approval from time to time.

By the time they'd exhausted the griffins—and Rolf—Celie was very pleased. They'd all learned some of the commands, and she was convinced that Rufus was a prodigy. He grasped the commands much faster than the others and was always ready to jump on Rolf when instructed. He was also older than the others, but she pushed that thought aside. Rufus was the best griffin, and that's all there was to it.

"I'm going to go show Pogue," she said, calling Arrow and Rufus to her with a flick of the wrist, a command they had just learned.

"Want me to come?" Rolf asked.

"If you want," Celie said, but she looked at Lilah as she said it. Juliet and Lorcan were curled up and looked like they might be falling asleep with the girls piled on top of them, so Lilah mouthed that she would be all right.

Celie hopped on Rufus, and Rolf got on Arrow's back and whistled for Dagger, which made Lorcan stir but not wake, fortunately. Together they flew down to the shipyard, thus avoiding having to call for a coach and footmen and possibly put on new clothes. It was much easier to do things with her brother, Rolf, than with pretty much anyone else she knew, except for Pogue, and she said as much when they landed.

"Ah, yes," Rolf said, nodding his head. "*Pogue.*"

"What about him?" Celie demanded.

"Oh, nothing," Rolf said innocently. "Except that you're getting to be very grown-up, and Pogue . . . well, here he comes," Rolf said, smothering a laugh with one hand.

Celie turned to look. Pogue was headed toward them, as Rolf had said, clapping for Arrow, who ran to greet his person. Pogue had his hair tied in a topknot the way the Grathian sailors did, and he had taken off his shirt in the heat. Celie felt her cheeks go warm.

She wasn't sure where to look as she told Pogue about the griffin training and put Arrow through his paces. Then Pogue offered to show them the work that had been done on the ship that day.

"If you recall," Rolf whispered as they followed Pogue to the ship, "I once predicted this would happen. And now it's going to be nothing but sighs and playing with your hair and Lilah teaching you how to flutter your eyelashes."

Celie's entire face was burning now. "Ugh," she said. "That's not . . . He's my friend!"

She jumped onto Rufus's back and flew up to the deck of the ship.

Chapter 6

The next day Lorcan was still very fractious, and Celie hardly dared to let him out of her sight. The others, too, were keeping their griffins close, in case they joined Lorcan in his mutiny. Instead of letting them fly out from the garden, they made them sit at their feet on the lawn, while the humans spoke nervously of what do to.

"The only thing to be doing is to be viewing the ship!" Orlath cried from the gate to the garden. "We are having such building as will make the finest of tours now!"

They all stood up, but were clearly not as enthusiastic as Orlath had hoped.

"But all is being grim," Orlath said, looking baffled. "All is being strange! But no! It cannot be such a thing! It is a time of shipbuilding! Of ship viewing! Of joy!"

"Of joy," Lilah echoed, sounding as though she didn't know the meaning of the word.

But once they were at the shipyard, the sight of their ship drove thoughts of Lulath's potentially dangerous mission from their minds. The ship truly was magnificent: rising high and proud on the shore of the harbor, distinctive from the other ships being built because of the variety of wood being used. The Grathian wood shone a light golden brown, while the Sleynth was a dark peat color, and the Arkish and Hathelocke parts gleamed reddish in the sun.

"A thing of the greatest beauty," Orlath said, throwing his arms wide.

The Glower family stood there and took it in, every inch of it. Celie was about to say something, to ask if it was supposed to look that way, when Pogue jogged over to them.

"I know, I know it's hideous," Pogue said. "I mean, I don't have much to compare it to, but from what the other men are saying, it's a monster cobbled together from old parts, and shouldn't even float." He grinned.

"What?" Lilah looked from Orlath to Pogue, her mouth open. "A monster? But what should we do? How do we fix it?"

"I like it," Rolf said as they all went closer to the ship. "It has . . . character."

"Of naturalness it will be sailing on the ocean with grace," Orlath said. "I am not knowing any other way of building such a ship!" He shook his head and laughed.

"But it is sure that this is being the only ship of its like to sail."

"It's perfect," Celie said at last, making up her mind.

And it was.

Care had been taken to preserve symmetry. There were just as many Sleynth planks as Grathian making up the hull, so that the ship had a striped appearance rather than one of patchwork, which Celie had privately feared. As they climbed the plank to the deck of the ship, they saw the brass instruments that had been taken from one of the towers in the Castle being mounted on swiveling stands. There was a stack of what Pogue told them were called belaying pins off to one side, waiting to be put along the sides of the ship for the sail ropes to be tied to. The pins were Hathelocke made, old, and of richly polished red wood, but the rails they would be set into were golden Grathian wood.

"It's perfect," Celie said again.

"I don't know," Lilah said, biting her lower lip. She pushed her heavy curls back from her face, a nervous gesture that almost—but not quite—dislodged her tiara. "What if they're right?"

"But, Lilah," Celie protested, "it's exactly what we wanted! It's a ship made of all the parts of all our lands!"

She windmilled her arms, trying to embrace the ship the way the Grathians always seemed to embrace any-thing that pleased them. But really, she was trying to cover up something: she felt it, too. The ship *wasn't* what it was supposed to be.

"I just don't know," Lilah said slowly.

"It's not alive," Rolf said bluntly. "It's not like the Castle." He rocked back on his heels, his thumbs in his belt.

"I was wondering about that," Pogue said. "I can't feel it myself, you know. But I wanted to ask one of you what you felt."

"But what is being happening?" Orlath said. "For it was a certainty that the very sticks of the wood in the shipyard are having the best effects on my our Glower family." He frowned around. "What is being done that it is gone to sleep now?"

"How do we wake the ship up?" Pogue said.

He and Orlath turned and looked at Celie. So did Lilah. And Rolf.

Celie just looked back.

"I'm not a wizard," she said finally. "And I'm not the Builder of the Castle."

"Yes, but—" Rolf began, but Celie cut him off.

"Don't you dare say the Castle loves me best," she told him. "This isn't the Castle! And you're the heir; the Castle loves you, too."

She didn't want to sound childish, but she was getting just a trifle annoyed with everyone turning to her all the time for answers. It made her feel stupid when she didn't have any. And how could she possibly have one in this case? She knew just as much about the building of the

Castle as they did, and she'd never even been on a ship before. She had no wisdom to offer.

"Why don't we show you around?" Pogue said. He waved a hand and started toward the upper deck without waiting to see if they would follow. "The wheel is from the Builder's original ship, as you know," he began.

And so they took a tour of the new ship. There were still things that weren't in place. The doors weren't hung, for instance, but they had been stood in the rooms that they belonged to. The mast wasn't in place, but was waiting on the hard-packed earth of the shipyard, beside the figurehead, which Pogue told them would be the next-to-last part of the ship added, the sails being the last.

Celie stood in the bow and stared down at the shipyard, trying to figure out what it was. What had made the Castle the *Castle*? What would make the ship the *Ship*?

Her eyes lit on the figurehead.

"Pogue," Celie called out.

"I'm one step ahead of you," Rolf crowed. "For once."

He leaped up onto the rail and balanced there. He clapped his hands to get the attention of the workers. When they were all looking at him, he cupped his hands to his mouth to make the announcement.

"I know it's not this way done in Grath," he said, in his best Grathian. "But we are be needing the head figure on the ship. Right now."

"Rolf, you're a genius," Lilah said.

"I thought of it, too," Celie muttered.

Pogue nudged her. "Let him have his moment," he whispered.

Celie made a face, but couldn't hold it. She wasn't really angry. The most important thing was that they get the figurehead in place.

That they get the figurehead in place, and that they turn out to be right: this *would* bring the ship to life.

Because that was the thing, what they'd all been hoping for since Celie had first found the figurehead in an unused room behind the nursery. No one had dared to say it, but they'd all been wishing it to be true, that the ship would become a live thing, like the Castle. It had been so reassuring to sit by the figurehead and watch the building of the ship this past week, but now that feeling of comfort was gone, and Celie was worried.

Of course, it would take some work to get the figurehead properly in place, but they all wanted to watch. It fitted under the jutting prow, and couldn't really be seen from on deck, so they filed down the plank to the ground again to wait. Stools were brought, and refreshments, and their griffins flew down to join them. It was almost like a picnic, except no one was talking and all eyes were on the gilded wooden griffin being carefully fitted to the bow of the ship.

The sky was darkening, and Lady Griffin had already delivered two messages from their mother reminding them to return to the Sanctuary in time to dress for dinner. But at last the final nail was hammered, and the figurehead was in place.

It was a thing of great beauty: a majestic griffin with wings upraised so that they swept back on either side of the bow. The rich wood was polished to a shine, and there were touches of gilt to bring out the fierce eyes and finely carved feathers.

"It's not ugly, it's beautiful," Lilah breathed.

She was right: the piecework look that had hung around the ship before was gone. The griffin completed the ship, though the mast and sails were not yet in place.

"Now this is being the very! The very ship!" Orlath said. He picked Lilah up and spun her around, presumably because the ship was too big to embrace.

"Not yet," Celie said under her breath.

Beside her, she could hear Rolf also muttering something. Was he counting? Praying? She wasn't sure. But he didn't have to count very high, or pray very long.

A great shudder ran through the ship. They could all see it. Several of the men working on the upper deck shouted and fell to their knees as every plank resettled itself. The figurehead appeared to stretch and then freeze again, looking exactly the same save for a slightly fiercer glint to its eyes, Celie thought.

"There it is," Rolf whispered.

"Like a bird ruffling its feathers," Celie agreed.

"Or a griffin," Pogue said in awe.

The men were scrambling to get off the ship, but the

Glower family and their friends paid them no mind. They all hurried to get *on* the ship, to see if there had been any changes.

Though there were no changes to be seen, none of the Glower children were disappointed. It was obvious from the moment they stepped onto the deck that the ship had come to life.

"It's like the Castle," Celie breathed. "We were right."

"What wonders!" Orlath cried. "The very nails did dance! Are you feeling a something?"

They were. It was exactly the way things were at home, something Celie never noticed until it was taken away. It was almost, but not quite, a vibration. Almost, but not quite, a sound. If you'd lived all your life with it, you would never notice it. But having spent the past weeks in the Sanctuary, Celie was acutely aware of the difference between the stones of Lulath's ancestral home and the planks of the ship's deck.

And so was Pogue.

His face was shining, and he looked around them in wonder.

"I can feel it," he said, entranced. "*I can feel it!*"

Back home at the Castle, only the Glower family could feel the Castle, and it reacted only to them. Celie knew this was a blow to Pogue and others who spent a great deal of time there, and who respected and loved the Castle and the Glowers. She had assumed there was something in her family's blood that made them part of the Castle.

But the look on Pogue's face said it all: he could feel the ship.

"This is amazing!" he said. "I can't believe it! I'm feeling the ship!"

"Well, I am not," Orlath said, sounding just a little cross. Then he grinned with pride. "But to be sure: it is a fine, fine ship."

"It's not *a* ship," Celie corrected him, also grinning. "It's *the* Ship."

Chapter
7

Do you think the Ship will be ready to sail by the night of the betrothal celebration?" Queen Celina asked, strolling across the deck the next morning.

"It is my thinking so," Orlath said. "But only for the very short sailings. Will these many parts be in harmony? I am not knowing—not at the first," he hastened to add. "It will be having small cruises of the harbor before there is the larger undertaking."

"Celie, aren't you excited?" Lilah whispered. "The Ship is almost finished!" She patted her hands together. "Lulath will be so happy when he gets back!"

"Um, yes . . . ?" Celie said, drawing her mind back to the present. "It's very nice."

"Nice?" Lilah arched an eyebrow. "It's a *Ship*. Can you imagine the look on Lulath's face when he feels it?"

"I know," Celie said, moving restlessly around in the bow, picking up and putting down a belaying pin. She hadn't slept well since Lulath had left to find the griffin rider village, though Lilah seemed to have moved from worry about him to anticipation of his return since the figurehead of the Ship had been put in place. "I—I just—"

"I know," Lilah said.

"You do?" she asked. "Oh, well, of course you do—"

"You're thinking I've forgotten about our quest," Lilah went on. "But I assure you I haven't! As a matter of fact, I have everything planned out."

Celie was baffled. "Our . . . quest?"

"To find the unicorns," Lilah said with impatience.

"Oh," Celie said.

"Listen," Lilah said, lowering her voice. "Have you noticed how Mother never mentions that anymore? How she only talks about building the Ship and then going back to Sleyne?"

Celie nodded. Although, really, from the beginning it had always been Lilah's quest, and no one else's.

"Well," Lilah said, drawing Celie even closer to the rail, "I'm not going to let my dream be set aside. We have plenty of time to go to the Land of a Thousand Waterfalls," she told her, using Larien's older, more romantic, name.

"All right," Celie said, not feeling even slightly romantic.

"What I'm planning," Lilah continued, not noticing Celie's lack of enthusiasm, "is to take the Ship out for one of these little harbor cruises that they're talking about, and then we demand that the Ship take us to Larien!"

Lilah tossed her hair back and waited for Celie's answer, but Celie didn't know quite what to say. It sounded like Lilah wanted to steal her own ship. But was that stealing? It was Lilah's and Lulath's ship together, to be exact, but would Lulath go along with this plan?

She asked this last question out loud.

"Lulath will do whatever I ask," Lilah said airily, but Celie thought she looked slightly worried.

"So you want to steal the Ship?" Celie said.

"It's not stealing if it belongs to me," Lilah said, answering that question at least—albeit in a very round-about way. "And I'm not going to *steal* it. I'm just going to make sure we have everyone and everything on board that we'll need for the journey, and then when we're out in the harbor, I'll simply command it."

"I see," Celie said.

"Don't you dare get cold feet," Lilah warned her.

"Me? This isn't *my* plan!" Celie protested.

"But you want to find the unicorns, too," Lilah said. "Don't you?"

Celie paused, but she wasn't really thinking about the answer. Of course she wanted to find the unicorns. She wanted to know that the griffins hadn't killed them all. She wanted to prove that they could live peacefully in Sleyne with the griffins.

And, to be honest with herself, Celie wanted to know what it would be like to have a pet unicorn.

"I've spent too much time around Lulath," Celie muttered.

"What's *that* supposed to mean?" Lilah said with a huff.

"It means, yes, I'll help you," Celie said.

Lilah squealed and hugged her.

"Calm down," Celie said, worried that someone would see and ask what Lilah was so excited about. "You don't want to let the cat out of the bag."

"The *unicorn* out of the bag," Lilah said gleefully.

"Unicorns?" Pogue asked, coming out of the hatch near their feet. "What unicorns?" He put a hand over his eyes for a moment. "Do I even want to know?"

"It's none of your concern," Lilah snapped.

"Lilah!" Celie said, as Pogue's face turned red.

"Oh, I would say that it is Pogue's concern," Queen Celina said. "I would say that it's all of our concern." She arched an eyebrow at Lilah. "First apologize to Pogue, and then tell us what this is about unicorns."

Chapter
8

⁓⊰≋⊱⁓

They fell into a routine over the next few days. In the mornings they would train their griffins in the garden, and in the afternoons they would go to the Ship and help wherever they could. Lilah developed a keen skill at coiling ropes, Celie learned how to hang doors on their hinges, and Rolf hammered anything that had not yet been hammered into place.

The griffins were kept out of trouble by having them fetch and carry things in baskets. The Grathian workers didn't like it at first, but they soon got used to the griffins, and even began to politely ask them for specific things in halting Sleynth.

"We should have this done right on schedule," Pogue told Celie as they hung the last door. "And Lilah will have her fireworks and her Ship together." He said it with a surprising lack of bitterness.

Celie looked at him. Before Lulath and Lilah had started whispering in corners and then declaring their undying love for each other, Pogue had hung around the Castle mostly to flirt with Lilah, and occasionally to get Rolf into (and then usually out of) trouble. When they'd been in Hatheland, Pogue had definitely been jealous of Lilah and Lulath's budding romance, but now he seemed indifferent.

Pogue saw the way Celie was looking at him and shrugged.

"Why shouldn't she marry Lulath and be happy?" he said. "I like Lulath."

"Everyone does," Celie agreed. "It would be hard not to. But—"

Pogue shook his head. "It was fun to be *in* love with Lilah," he told her. "But I don't actually love Lilah. I mean, not like that." He made a face. "I mean, she's much smarter than I think we all give her credit for. But she's a *princess*. She needs to marry a prince like Lulath, and not a blacksmith turned knight."

"Turned griffin rider," Celie said, slotting the last hinge into place.

"Thank you," Pogue said. "Yes, and a griffin rider."

"Mummy and Daddy wouldn't have cared if it had been you and not Lulath who wanted to marry Lilah," Celie told him, though she wasn't entirely sure about that.

Maybe they would have. They had been awfully

pleased that Lilah was marrying into the wealthy and powerful Grathian royal family. But it didn't matter now.

"I'm just happy for Lilah that she's going to marry someone she loves," Pogue said, picking up the spare odds and ends and putting them in a basket. "I hope you get to do the same."

Celie didn't have a reply for that. She hadn't ever thought about it much, although she knew Rolf had. Everyone knew that her parents had been sealed up together in a room by the Castle itself, in order to steer them into a betrothal. Celie wasn't sure which worried Rolf more: that the Castle would choose a wife for him, or that their parents would do it.

But now she was worried about herself. What if the Castle chose someone for her whom she didn't even know? Or what if the Castle *didn't*? Would her parents choose someone for her? Some unknown prince from Bendeswe? A distant lord from Sleyne City?

"Forget I said anything," Pogue said, looking at her in alarm.

"Why would you say that to me?" Celie demanded as they returned the basket of bits and pieces to the head carpenter and waited for another assignment. "I'm never going to be able to think of anything else!"

"Why, what are we thinking about?" Rolf said, putting down his hammer and stretching. "Is it that weird, spongy sea-something that was in the soup last night? I know

I can't stop thinking about how often they serve that, and whether there's a polite way to refuse."

"No," Celie said.

"Yes," Pogue said at the same time. "We're talking about food," he added.

"What *was* that last night?" Rolf said, making a face. "It wasn't a fish. It wasn't a bird. It was all squishy and . . . chewy." He shuddered.

"I fed mine to JouJou," Celie admitted, glad to change the subject. "I feed a *lot* of my food to JouJou."

"That's ingenious," Rolf said. "I'm going to have to get a dog to sit in my lap during meals!"

"That shouldn't be hard," Pogue said. "Plenty to choose from."

"Why do you think JouJou likes me so much?" Celie said with amusement. "I've been doing this since Lulath came to the Castle!"

"You little sneak," Rolf said in admiration. "But what do *you* eat?"

"Well," Celie said, "this may be the reason why the kitchen staff at the Castle—and now the Sanctuary—think griffins live on bread, cheese, apples, and custard."

"My hat goes off to you," Rolf said. "If I had a hat, it would, that is."

"Have you not a hat?" Orlath came over to them. "Is it being stolen?" He looked anxious.

"Um, no . . ." Rolf said. "I just . . . it's just a saying, I suppose."

"Ah, well, my Jocko is being the worst of thieves," he said, feeding a nut to the monkey on his shoulder. "If ever you are having something stolen, please be telling me. I will see if this bad boy has it."

"The griffins love shiny things," Celie told him. "So if it's jewelry and it's not Jocko, we'll check the griffins' beds."

"So like being birds," Orlath marveled as they watched Arrow soar overhead, bringing a bucket of tar to one of the men.

"I can't tell how much of their behavior is like a lion's," Celie said. "I've never seen a lion in real life."

"Well," Orlath said, "be coming with me on a journey, and there will—"

"Is that Lady Griffin?" Celie said, interrupting him.

She didn't mean to, and she apologized a second later, but by that time they could all see Lady Griffin winging her way toward them. They all paused to watch as the queen of the griffins landed neatly on the deck just in front of them. She turned her back to them and looked over her shoulder, so that they could see a scroll tucked into her harness.

Rolf took it and unrolled it.

"Lulath's back," he said.

"Is he all right?" Celie asked.

"It just says he's back," Rolf said.

They all exchanged looks.

"Lilah!" Celie shouted. "Lilah! Lulath's back!"

They heard a squawking that sounded like something that might come from a griffin, and Lilah came up from below deck. She looked around wildly.

"He's at the Sanctuary," Rolf explained.

"Juliet!" Lilah cried.

Instantly her griffin was there. Lilah leaped onto her back. Celie and the others all whistled for their griffins and followed her.

They flew straight for the courtyard, where there were horses and coaches milling about. In the middle of it all stood Lulath, in perfect health.

As soon as Juliet's talons hit the pavement, Lilah was off her back and leaping at Lulath. He caught her easily, laughing, and they kissed. Then he put her down, and they stood there blushing while everyone else gathered around.

"What did they say?" Rolf demanded.

Lulath's brow clouded. "They are saying to me nothing."

"They still wouldn't talk to you?" Pogue frowned. "Did they let you into the village?"

"There was no person to stop our going in," Lulath said. "Of the village there is only houses, empty as shells on this very beach.

"The people, they are being long gone."

Chapter
9

By the night of the betrothal celebration, they still hadn't found any sign of the villagers. From what Lulath and the others of his party could tell, the village had been abandoned a year ago or more, and any tracks had long since been washed away.

Celie had been having nightmares that the missing villagers were watching them from within the walls of the Sanctuary, as Wizard Arkwright had been in the Castle. King Kurlath had assured the Glower family that there were no hidden passages in the Sanctuary, but still Celie felt every wall and floor tile in her room. She poked every inch of every ornamental doorway and pulled the books off every shelf, but it seemed true that there were no secret passages.

Lulath's family had built the Sanctuary, and there had never been a war fought on Grathian soil. So as the king kindly pointed out to Celie, there was no need for them to have any secret hiding places.

Queen Celina had shared Celie's suspicions at first, but once the Royal Wizard had helped her perform a spell that found no sign of any of the villagers anywhere in the area, she, too, believed them to be gone.

"They could be anywhere," Queen Celina admitted. "But they're not here in the Sanctuary, that's certain. Perhaps they gave up hope of having griffins again and left."

"But left to go *where?*" Rolf said plaintively.

"Wherever they like," Queen Celina countered. "I think they were waiting for something to happen, all these years in their village. The return of the griffins, most likely. It happened, and it had nothing to do with them, so they left."

This wasn't all that reassuring, but it was all they had, so they continued with their preparations for the betrothal. Lilah and Lulath would not marry for another year, of course, but in the meantime their intention to marry needed to be shouted to the skies, and, more important, to the Grathians.

The betrothal celebration was to be the most wonderful thing anyone had ever seen, according to Queen Amatopeia. Lilah and Lulath would be married in Sleyne, but for the first time, Celie understood Lilah's constant worry that their family would look poor in front of Lulath's.

The betrothal festivities would last from dawn until the following dawn, and Celie herself had five changes of clothing for the event, beginning with a breakfast gown and ending with a ship-launching gown. All of these were delivered to her room the night before, along with a maid who had been assigned to dress her in each ensemble, fix her hair, and follow her around to make any needed repairs or adjustments.

At first Celie was annoyed by both the costume changes and the assignment of the maid, but it turned out to be the most fun she'd had in ages.

For one thing, the food was delicious, which made up for a lot of the fuss.

Then the clothes turned out to fit perfectly (which might have been achieved through magic, as Celie had not been measured or fitted by anyone in Grath).

The maid, Renia, was a good-humored girl a few years older than Celie, whose duties not only included changing Celie's clothes and hair but also carrying things like fans and gloves, which Celie was always dropping or losing. Renia even had a small flask of hot chocolate hanging from her belt, in case Celie need a little refreshment. And she wasn't afraid of Rufus, either. After meeting the griffin, Renia added a pouch of biscuits to her accoutrements just for him, which endeared her to both Celie and Rufus forever.

The first breakfast took place in the larger, more formal gardens. Everyone lay on couches to eat, and the servants placed tiny plates on low tables by the side of each couch. The Glower family and Lulath's family weren't to move around, but the rest of the court and ambassadors from various countries came to bow to them, and perhaps share a slice of cake or melon.

Rolf thought this was the most amazing thing he'd ever seen, and he lounged across his couch and dropped food into his mouth with abandon.

Pogue came over to talk to them, and laughed so hard at Rolf that he ended up sitting on the end of Celie's couch to recover. A servant instantly brought Pogue his own tray, and he spent the rest of the breakfast with Celie, throwing food at Rolf when no one was looking, and at Arrow and Rufus even when they were. The dogs had been locked inside the Sanctuary for the occasion, but JouJou managed to get out, and Celie propped her in the crook of her arm and fed her cake until the little dog fell asleep. When JouJou began snoring, a servant appeared with a velvet cushion and bore her away, as though he were carrying the king's crown.

"This isn't another country," Pogue said. "It's another *world*!"

"And it is only being the more fantastical," Lulath called out. "After, there is being a parade! With all the darlings!" He clapped his hands. "And a parade of boats in the later, when there has been more food."

"How is it possible for there to be more food?" Rolf groaned. "I think I have cake coming out of my ears."

"That's what you get for making a pig of yourself," Lilah said.

She said it very pleasantly, though, without losing her smile, because the ambassador from Bendeswe was hovering near her couch, and fortunately he did not speak Sleynth. She and Lulath had a sort of V-shaped double couch to lounge on, and he laughed and put some grapes in her mouth.

"It is being expected," he said. "Therefore there are being also parades!"

"What sort of parades?" Celie asked.

In Sleyne they sometimes had a springtime parade, when the village children would dress as birds and flowers and butterflies and dance down the main road to the Castle. And sometimes the guards would put on their nicest uniforms and parade in the courtyard, to show their training off to the king. But Lulath had a twinkle in his eye—more so than usual.

"Wait and be seeing, our Celie," he said.

The parade required a change of clothes, which included a very stiff but slightly short gown that made Celie feel like she was wearing a bell, and some beautifully embroidered leather shoes with sturdy soles. Renia put a large bow around Rufus's neck, made from the same blue satin as Celie's gown, and produced a square sunshade that hung from a curved shaft, like a wilting flower, which she said she would hold over Celie during the parade.

"What kind of parade is it?" Celie asked her.

"It's for the people," was all the maid replied. "But there's lunch afterward," she said, in the manner of one offering a reward.

Celie groaned. Renia had barely been able to lace her into the parade gown. Although Celie hadn't been quite as gluttonous as Rolf, she had eaten a fair amount at breakfast.

The parade consisted of the Grathian royal family and the Glower family, along with their closest associates, walking through the city with all their darlings, as Lulath had said. That meant over two dozen people (Lulath's siblings and their spouses had come for the celebration), almost a dozen griffins, two dozen parrots, a monkey, and an army of small dogs, with servants holding sunshades, marching through the city.

"This is horrible," Rolf moaned.

"That's what you get for eating your own weight in cake," Lilah told him, still smiling and barely moving her lips.

She was waving to her new people, and they were chanting her name. It was impossible not to cheer for Lilah. She was wearing a red gown that matched Lulath's tunic, and it was the perfect color for her. It brought out the roses in her cheeks and the lights in her blue eyes. Her dark curly hair had been pomaded to shine even more, and she wore a pearl-studded tiara given to her by Queen Amatopeia. Young men blew her kisses, and small girls in their best gowns ran out of the crowd to hand her bouquets. She blushed on cue and thanked them graciously.

"See that?" Pogue whispered, sticking his head under Celie's sunshade. "That's why she's better off married to Lulath."

Just then a young girl handed Celie a bouquet, and her giggling older sister tossed a circle of daisies at Rolf, ringing him perfectly around the neck. She blew him a kiss, and Celie burst out laughing.

"You look like the prize bull at the fair," she told him.

"I have more flowers than you," Rolf teased. Sure enough, there were three flower chains around his neck, and he was starting to strut. "I rather like this. We should all marry Grathians. The food is excellent, and pretty girls give you flowers." He sneezed, then sneezed again.

"You should give those purple ones to Pogue," Queen Celina said dryly, "before your eyes swell up and no one wants to give you anything."

He hastily took off the purple garland and tried to hand it to Pogue. Pogue warded him off.

"They don't match my tunic," he said with a laugh.

"Here," Celie said, worried that Rolf's eyes would swell up and spoil the day for him. She took the wreath and hung it around Rufus's neck.

That started a positive mania for giving the griffins flowers. Which was a relief, because Celie didn't think she could carry any more. The more daring children would come right up to the griffins, who would hold very still and bow their heads for the flowers to be put around their necks. The shy children would present a person with the flowers but whisper, "Griffin." And Celie and the others would thank them and hang their gift off the griffins' necks or harnesses.

There were smaller wreaths for the dogs, and also treats offered. Celie wondered if someone might try to steal one, or if a dog would go into the crowd after a treat and get lost. She caught up to King Kurlath, at the head of the parade, and asked him if it was safe for the dogs.

"Oh, my dear little princess," he told her in Grathian. "Just watch!"

Sure enough, a moment later a small black-and-white dog dove into the crowd after a child who was covered in something sticky and delicious. The boy picked up the dog, let it lick his face, and then gently set it back in the pack streaming by.

"The royal dogs are known," King Kurlath said in Grathian. "None would dare to steal one! And if they are lost, all know where they are to be returned. We give puppies away quite often, and not only to the court. One need only apply with the steward, and one may be considered the next time there is a litter."

A little girl ran forward and gave the king a biscuit that looked as if she'd been clutching it a little too tightly in her fist. The king took the biscuit and ate it with every appearance of delight. He held the girl's hand and had her walk along beside him for a bit while he praised her baking. Her father came to collect her, bowing. The king kissed the girl's cheek, and they faded back into the cheering crowd, smiling.

"This is why there's never been a war in Grath," Queen Celina whispered, coming up on Celie's other side. "Who would dare attack such a king?"

"Who would want to?" Celie agreed. "He'd probably give them a puppy and win them right over."

"I'm sure if the situation were serious enough, he'd give them at least two dogs," Queen Celina said.

"And a parrot," added Celie.

Chapter
10

⌒≈⌒

They were all more than ready for lunch after that, which was served at long tables in the center of the city. The king heard petitions as they ate, and people came forward to wish Lilah and Lulath well and to bow to the rest of the Glowers. Then they were taken in coaches back to the Sanctuary to change for the boat parade.

The boat parade was not unlike the first parade, except the animals had to stay behind, and they were rowed in boats along the river outside the city instead of walking. The people of the farms who hadn't been able to come into the city gathered along the shore and cheered and threw flowers as they sailed along. They went all the way to the mouth of the river, where it emptied into the harbor. There it seemed that every sailor on every Grathian ship and every dockworker had gathered to cheer for them. King Kurlath made a speech thanking them all for being the backbone of Grathian trade, and inviting them to the launching of the Ship at dawn the next day. More cheers, and then more coaches back to the Sanctuary.

There Celie took a much-needed nap before being dressed in her first ball gown.

It was green and had gold lace, and she hated to admit it, but she loved it. It made her feel like a real princess, instead of just a girl who happened to live in a castle.

The bodice had stays in it, so that she had to stand very upright, and the sleeves weren't puffy or ruffled or otherwise silly but long and embroidered and trimmed with lace. Renia piled Celie's curly blond hair on top of her head and carefully pinned it so that it wouldn't come down during the dancing. She set Celie's crown on her head and then pinned that in some secret way so it didn't move, either. Celie was going to have to find out how she did that.

Rufus was supposed to be with her, but he refused to budge from the room when Celie tried to leave. He kept going over to the dressing table and making gargling noises.

"What is it, you silly beast?" Celie asked with impatience. She was eager to show off her gown.

"Your Highness?" Renia ventured. "Do you think he wants . . . another bow?"

Rufus squawked in approval, and Celie started laughing. While Renia found a green ribbon, Celie brushed Rufus's fur and ran a silk handkerchief over his feathers to make them gleam. Renia tied a big bow atop his harness and put one of the fresher-looking garlands around his neck. Preening, he went straight to the door, ready for dinner and the ball.

Celie and Renia were still laughing when they reached the back hall where the rest of her family was waiting. Queen Celina gasped when she saw Celie, and Rolf let out a whistle. She'd almost forgotten about the new grown-up gown, and wasn't sure what was wrong for a moment.

"Oh," she said. "Do you like it?" She did a slow turn.

"Oh, my little girl," Queen Celina said. She put out her hand and just brushed Celie's cheek. Her eyes were uncharacteristically misty. "Look at you."

"I honestly thought you were one of Lulath's cousins," Rolf said admiringly. "You should dress like that all the time."

Celie ruined the effect by sticking out her tongue at him. She felt that she had to do something to make everyone stop staring at her.

"I'm, um . . . I'm your escort," Pogue said, clearing his throat.

"But just going into the ball," Lilah said briskly. "After that, Orlath is your escort for the rest of the evening. You'll sit beside him at dinner, and he'll lead you into the first dance."

Lilah looked Celie over with a critical eye. "Just as I thought," she said with great satisfaction. "The perfect style and color for you. And Renia is wonderful with hair." She beamed at the girl, who curtsied. "We should see if she'll return to Sleyne with us."

Lilah, of course, looked perfect. She was wearing pink with slashes of red and the same gold lace that decorated Celie's gown, and their mother's. She had her official crown on, and her hair was caught up in the back in a gold net studded with rubies. When Lulath arrived a moment later, he was in red with gold lace, and he feigned a swoon at the sight of them all.

"My glorious Lilah! My vision of greatest beauty!" he cried. "My noble queen-mother-to-be, a sorcerous vision of her own self!" And then he saw Celie and raised both hands in the air. "This is not my our Celie? This is the magnificent being that has come before us?"

Celie felt herself turning red. "I like your coat," she told him. "The gold buttons are very fancy."

"Oh, such thanks," he said. "Now, friend Sir Pogue! Are you not being almost as full of luck as I?"

"Celie looks very nice," Pogue said, taking her arm in an awkward way.

"Yes, she does," Lilah said, looking at him with narrowed eyes.

But Queen Celina smiled. She raised Pogue's arm slightly and positioned Celie's hand atop his elbow. "Very nice," she said. "You'll come after Rolf and me, and we'll go in after Lilah and Lulath."

They lined up, and Arrow and Rufus came to stand on either side of Pogue and Celie. Pogue noticed Rufus's ribbon and garland and relaxed a little, laughing.

"Don't let Arrow see; he'll be jealous," he said. "I had to fight him to get the flowers off his harness after the parade."

"Mean!" Celie said. "You should have left them! He looked so *pretty*."

That got a laugh out of Pogue, and a hiss from Lilah at the front of the line. They were standing in front of a pair of broad double doors, each carved with a giant clamshell. A pair of footmen threw open the doors, and they were greeted with a great wave of cheers.

They walked into the ballroom, where the court and all the dignitaries were gathered. There was music, and servants carrying trays of tiny foods, and a hundred thousand people to meet. After a dizzying hour of name after name and curtsy after curtsy—as though they hadn't spoken with many of the same people at the breakfast, and the parade, and the lunch, and the other parade— Celie finally had her hand passed from Pogue's supportive arm to Orlath's and was led into dinner.

Pogue was seated some way down the table, surrounded by royal cousins, all of them tall and golden-haired and very merry. But since Celie had been working with Orlath for a couple of weeks now, they had had quite a good time making further plans for the Ship. Orlath told her all about the launch the next day as well, and she could hardly wait.

The food was sumptuous and plentiful. And there were many toasts to the betrothed pair, who sat on a double seat at the head of the table, with the king sitting on Lulath's right hand, and Queen Celina on Lilah's left. At one point, carried away in the moment, Celie stood and toasted Lilah and Lulath in Grathian, saying that Lulath had become as dear as a brother over their adventures together.

Everyone cheered as she sat back down with a groan.

"Did I really just say that Lilah is my *favorite* sister?" she asked Orlath in a whisper.

"Yes. Why?" he whispered back.

"She's my *only* sister," Celie whispered in mortification.

Orlath roared with laughter. When Celie finally dared to look down the table, she saw that Lilah was busy chatting with the king, and no one appeared to have noticed her mistake. She relaxed, and then had to giggle a little as well.

And then came the dancing.

Grathian dances were also quite the fashion in Sleyne, and Celie and her siblings had been taught by an excellent dancing master, who had started drilling them in jigs and roundelays from the minute they could walk. She and Orlath were able to swan about the ballroom with the rest of the royal party with great skill.

Orlath was a wonderful dancer, despite the monkey

clinging to his shoulder. Jocko had not been present during dinner, since he apparently had a bad habit of stealing food and throwing it at people, half-chewed. But he scampered in as soon as they entered the ballroom, and Celie danced with him snatching at her hair all the while.

She danced with King Kurlath, with Rolf, and with Lulath and all the rest of his brothers. She even danced with Pogue, though at the end of the dance she had to tell him he was not a very good dancer. She couldn't help it: it was almost a relief to find something Pogue wasn't good at, and to break up the strange stiffness that had overtaken him that evening.

After the dancing there were fireworks. Celie had heard tell of them, but had never seen anything more exciting than the little red "snappers" that the village boys loved to buy from traveling peddlers. They made a loud bang and a puff of smoke when you lit them, which wasn't that exciting after the first scare.

These were something else entirely. The court gathered on the terrace outside the ballroom, overlooking the sea, and gazed up at the sky.

At first there was nothing to look at except the velvety sky, studded with stars like the jewels that glittered on the members of the court. And then a flower made of pink fire exploded above them. There were trailing golden comets, and scarlet wheels, and little blue stars that sizzled before they winked out. The fireworks lit the faces of the people watching, painting them with glorious lights, and Celie thought she had never seen anything more wonderful in her life.

The griffins, however, did not care for fireworks. When the first flower ascended, they all howled in fright and ran back into the ballroom. Queen Celina gave a quick order to Lady Griffin, who seemed the least frightened, to keep the others there, and then had the servants shut the doors to the terrace. After a while, Rufus and Lorcan objected to being cut off from their people and crawled back out. Lorcan cowered behind Lulath, and Rufus began to squawk and carry on until Celie took the shawl that Renia had brought her and wrapped it around his head. Orlath's monkey was hiding inside his master's coat, and none of the dogs were in sight, either.

It seemed that fireworks were best admired by people, and really, that was fine by Celie. She enjoyed every second of them, and sighed with regret when the sky turned dark once more.

She sighed with regret again when her mother told her it was time to retire for the night. She would have protested, but it seemed that everyone was dispersing, and it was not just that Celie was being sent off to bed because of her age.

"You'll thank me in a few hours, when it's time for breakfast," Queen Celina said as they all made their way to their rooms.

"A few hours?" Rolf groaned. "What time is it now?"

"It's three hours to dawn," the queen said. "And dawn is—"

"The launching of the Ship!" Celie said.

"Just so," her mother said. "Apparently it's been moved to the docks, and we'll have breakfast on board after we give it a name and launch it properly."

Celie thought she would be too excited about the launch to sleep, but she'd also been the length and breadth of the city that day, not to mention dancing several more miles at the ball. As soon as Renia had her in her shift, Celie fell facedown on the bed.

"I'm just going to lie here for a moment," Celie said. Rufus cuddled up beside her.

The next thing she knew, Renia was gently shaking her shoulder.

"I'm sorry, Your Highness," the maid was saying, "but it's time to get dressed for breakfast and the ship naming."

"What?" Celie rolled over. "Where am I?"

Renia laughed and gently tugged her upright.

It took Celie a few minutes to wake up fully. She splashed water on her face for far longer than normal, and Renia had to feed her toast and hot chocolate before she could really think. Then Celie had to rush into her final gown, with Renia's help. This gown was simpler in cut but the same striking shade of green as Celie's ball gown. Her hair was still stiff from the pomade of the night before, but Renia managed to twist it back and get Celie's crown seated comfortably all the same.

Then Rufus wanted a bow, and Renia had to collect all the gloves and fans and things that she thought Celie would need. At last, though, they were on their way. In the corridor they bumped into the rest of the Glower family, who all looked equally sleepy, with the exception of Lilah.

"It's time," she kept saying feverishly. "It's time!"

"What are we naming the Ship, anyway?" Rolf wanted to know. "The Builder's Ship doesn't sound very impressive, unless you know who the Builder is, and even then . . . meh."

"I think that name lacks a certain something," Queen Celina agreed. "Unless, of course, that's what you and Lulath have your hearts set on, darling."

"No, no," Lilah assured them. "I've seen the Builder's *dead body*. I don't really want to think of that every time I set foot on the deck of *my* Ship."

"What? Am I not also having this Ship?" Lulath demanded as they met him in the entrance hall.

He swung Lilah around and kissed her. It came as a surprise to no one that he was wide-awake and looked completely refreshed. His parents also looked bright-eyed and ready for the day as they all climbed into the waiting coaches.

Once they were at the docks, with the brisk air blowing on their cheeks, Celie also felt more alert. The sky was just beginning to lighten, and there was a large gathering of people there to see the naming.

The Ship looked beautiful in the growing light. The wood gleamed, and the blue and red sails were very striking, as was the design of their unusual ship. A length of white canvas had been draped down each side of the bow to hide the name that had been painted on late last night.

Celie felt rather pettish about this. Lilah and Lulath had agreed on a name, and then told no one . . . except the crew and anyone who happened to walk by while the name was being painted! Could they not have slipped a word into the ear of the family?

"Do you know?" she whispered to Pogue as they stood and waited.

"No," he said. "And Lulath painted it on himself, I believe. Sometime after the second parade and before dinner."

"Well," Celie said, feeling slightly better. "I'm very curious, is all."

"I'll lay you a gold crown it's called the Rainbow Unicorn," Rolf whispered on Celie's other side.

Pogue snorted.

"She wouldn't," Celie breathed in horror.

"Have you met our sister?" Rolf demanded.

Lilah glared at them, and then it was time. The sun rose, making the golden accents of the ship catch fire.

King Kurlath made a speech, which was mostly thanking Celie's father for giving them a ship as a gift. Then Queen Celina stepped forward and protested very formally that it was their pleasure. Much to Celie's pleasure, Queen Celina also had Celie come forward, and explained that it was Celie who had found the figurehead, and how she had assisted in building the Ship. Then she thanked Pogue for taking charge, as well as Orlath, and everyone cheered and bowed, and then Lilah, who looked very pale, came forward.

Lilah also thanked everyone: her parents, Lulath's parents, and those who had worked on the Ship. Lulath joined her, but he merely waved, causing more cheers. Then a priest came forward and said a blessing. He handed them a bottle of pure rainwater.

Holding it together, Lilah and Lulath smashed the bottle on the side of the ship as the priest said another prayer, imploring the gods to see the Ship always returned safe to harbor, as rain returns to the sea.

As they smashed the glass, crewmen on the upper deck let the canvas drop, revealing the Ship's name. At the same time, Lilah and Lulath shouted it together.

"The Golden Griffin!"

Chapter 11

⟨≈⟩

"This brilliant name is being all the thoughts of my Lilah," Lulath said later, as the two royal families, plus Pogue and various griffins and dogs, sat on the deck for breakfast. "As soon as it is being said to us, you two, you happy two, are having the naming of the ship, my Lilah is saying to me that it is being *The Golden Griffin!*"

They all raised glasses of fruit juice in Lilah's honor.

"It just seemed right," Lilah said demurely.

"Very much so," Queen Celina said. "I can't think of a more perfect name."

"I really thought it would be something about unicorns or puppies," Rolf admitted. "I've never been so glad to be wrong."

Lilah made a face at him.

"Well!" Orlath pushed himself back from the table. "Are we being ready?"

"Ready for what?" Celie asked.

She also got to her feet. She was ready for anything. Especially if it had to do with the Ship. Her heart started to pound.

"Is it time?" she asked Orlath. "Should we go?"

"Go where?" Queen Celina said, putting down her napkin.

"Anywhere," Celie said, holding out her arms. "It's a ship!"

"Anywhere in the harbor, correct?" Queen Celina said, looking from Celie to Lilah with a single eyebrow raised.

"Of course," Orlath said. "We must first test this magnificent Ship. We will take a simple cruise around the harbor to celebrate the betrothal and to test the soundness of the Ship!"

"A thing of great fineness," King Kurlath said, getting to his feet and reaching out a hand to his queen. "And a thing that you must all be enjoying your own selves."

"Oh, you are not going to sail with us?" Lilah said with disappointment.

"My our dear Lilah," Queen Amatopeia said. "It is being a very great secret that you must now be knowing." She looked around the table, very grave. They all stared back, suddenly silent.

"Here we are being a people of the sea," Queen Amatopeia said. "A people of the trading, and the ships." She shook her head sadly. "And my very Kurlath and I myself . . . we are being the sickest of seasicknesses. Were we to be going even unto this harbor, it would be this all the very time!" And then she made a highly indelicate vomiting sound.

Everyone stared at the elegant queen for a heartbeat. And then Rolf positively roared with laughter.

"Did you *really* just do that?" he demanded.

Queen Amatopeia looked pleased.

"Oh, my queen, you are being the most very!" King Kurlath laughed. "But"—he held up a cautionary finger—"she is also saying a truth. Even still do the insides of me go to and fro, as they went to and fro this yesterday at the river!" He shook his head. "Were they to go to and fro at this harbor, there would soon be to, and never fro!"

Rolf had to put his head down on the table. "That's the second best thing I've ever heard," he said in a muffled voice. He raised his head. "I'm going to use that some time, if I may, Your Majesty," he told the king. "If this coach hits one more pothole . . . I might to and not fro. . . . The perfect thing to say in such a situation!"

Now it was King Kurlath's turn to look pleased. He bowed to Rolf. "Be using it! Be using it with often times!"

"You really won't come?" Queen Celina asked, her brow furrowed.

But they insisted that they would not, and they took their leave with many hugs and kisses. They also gave orders to Orlath not to take too long, for although the betrothal celebration was now officially over, there was a family dinner that night, and possibly more dancing. If they were not too tired. This last was said in a tone that implied that the king could not imagine not wanting to dance all night, and Celie helped herself to another muffin as fortification against the day to come.

They saw the king and queen back across the gangplank to the dock, along with most of the servants. At Rolf's request they left breakfast there, in case he, like Celie, wanted more. But finally it was just the Glower family, Orlath, Lulath, and Pogue, along with the griffins and Lulath's girls. They all looked around in anticipation.

"And the now?" Orlath asked, flexing his fingers. "Are we being ready the now?"

"So the ready!" Lulath told him. "So the now!"

"Ready and waiting," Lilah said.

"Let's go!" Celie cheered.

The gangway was removed, and the ropes were cast off. Sailors ran back and forth on the deck, reeling in the ropes and getting the sails ready. Celie went to the helm to stand beside the huge wheel with Orlath. Pogue did, too, but the others went to the bow where they would have the best view.

Celie didn't care about the view. She wanted a chance to steer the Ship.

Orlath brought them about, as he called it, turning the Ship from the docks and letting it glide around the edge of the harbor. The wind was perfect, and so was the tide, he told them, and Pogue and Celie nodded obediently. Both of them had their hands behind their backs, trying not to clutch at the wheel themselves.

Orlath sensed this and continued to narrate everything he did. He showed them how the sails were brought down, and how the ropes were used to adjust them so that they caught the wind just right. He showed them how the turn of the great wheel moved the rudder so that the ship would go the direction you wanted.

As they approached the mouth of the harbor, Orlath turned to Celie.

"And now, Princess Celie?"

Celie didn't need to be asked twice. She grasped one of the handles sticking up from the wheel and held it just as she'd seen Orlath do. The wheel was warm and smooth under her hands, and it felt wonderful. She knew that Pogue was disappointed, and that he wanted to take a turn, but she didn't care. He could wait.

And then the wheel lurched to the side, and the boom swung to the side, shifting the main sail. The Ship began to leave the harbor mouth, rather than sailing past it and back around to the docks. Celie tried to turn the wheel, but it was too heavy.

"Ah, ah, ah!" Orlath said, laughing. "Not yet!" He took hold of the wheel on either side of Celie's hands and tried to turn it. It wouldn't budge. He grunted.

Pogue, seeing how Orlath was straining, also grabbed the wheel and tried to help them turn it, but still it would not move. The Ship began to sail out of the harbor with growing speed.

Several of the crew came forward, calling out to Orlath to find out if there had been a change of plans. He ordered them to reef the sails so that they would lose the wind and stop their progress, and they began to bustle about.

Lilah and Lulath hurried to the upper deck, concern written on both their faces.

"What are you doing?" Lilah asked, staring at the three of them trying to turn the wheel. "We're not supposed to leave the harbor!"

"Something's caught the rudder I think," Orlath grunted, speaking Grathian in his concern.

"Oh, no," Lilah said. "Is that bad? Is the Ship broken?"

"Oh, hardly," Orlath assured her. "We just have to get it into the dock and look."

There was sweat running down his face now as he tried to steer the Ship, but to no avail. There was sweat running down Pogue's and Celie's faces as well, and Celie's arms were shaking with the strain. It was like trying to move the Castle by pushing on one of the walls, and she said as much aloud.

"May I?" Lilah said.

She took over from Celie, and Lulath took over from his brother, standing shoulder to shoulder at the wheel of their Ship. The wheel didn't budge.

They heard a sailor swear, and looked to where the men were trying to get the sails down. But the ropes were whipping this way and that, slipping out of the men's hands as though taunting them.

"It's like trying to move the Castle," Celie repeated.

Pogue looked at her sharply. Rolf and Queen Celina had joined them now, and the queen appeared more thoughtful than concerned. Rolf just looked excited.

"Are we off to sea, then?" he said. "Excellent!"

"We're trying not to be," Lilah said from between gritted teeth. "There's something stuck on the rudder."

"Is there?" Queen Celina said. "Are you sure?"

"What is it, Mummy?" Celie asked.

"If you would be so kind as to tell the men to stop trying to reef the sails," Queen Celina instructed Orlath.

"Of course, madam," he said. He looked confused, but he called out the order anyway.

The men were also confused, but they let go of the ropes, which had continued to slip out of their fingers as soon as they were captured. Several of the men had climbed into the rigging, but now they dropped back down to the main deck.

The sails adjusted themselves. The ends of the ropes whipped around the belaying pins and tied themselves fast. The men shouted and prayed, and many of them fell to their knees.

"I think you can let go of the wheel now," Queen Celina said, looking rather grim.

"What's happening?" Orlath's voice was hushed.

"The Ship is taking us where it wants to go," Queen Celina said. "And I suppose we'd better let it."

Although Orlath was the captain of the Ship, which actually belonged to Lulath and Lilah, it was Queen Celina who took charge then. Well, the Ship had taken charge, but the queen took care of the people on board.

She ordered the food left from breakfast to be gathered up and stored properly, in case they needed it later. Then she had the cook check the other provisions that were on board and report back to her. They did, in fact, have enough food and water for a little over two weeks, he told Queen Celina, though he didn't look happy about it.

None of the crew did. They had rapidly left the harbor behind, and now they reluctantly unfurled the sails to find that the wind was in their favor. They were on the open sea, and though it was calm and the sun was shining, they didn't know where they were going, and they hadn't known that they would be leaving that day. No one had any spare clothes, and the crew's families were all expecting them home for dinner.

In the huddle around the helm they discussed ferrying the crew back to the docks on griffin-back, but it would take several trips, and most of the crew would not be too keen on riding a griffin. Not to mention the fact that if the Ship wanted to take them somewhere, they really should see where it was. The Castle had never done anything to hurt the Glower family, and Queen Celina told them that she had no doubt that the Ship felt the same way toward them.

"What do you think, Celie?" Lilah asked. "What do you think the Ship wants?"

"It's your Ship," Celie pointed out. "Maybe it's trying to make you happy."

Lilah blinked, and then her mouth dropped open. She looked from Celie to Lulath and then out at the open sea before them. She laid one hand on the wheel, and a smile slowly spread over her face.

"We're going to find the unicorns," Lilah whispered.

"Oh, good *heavens*," their mother said in despair. "Unicorns again!"

Chapter 12

Upon consultation with the Ship's crisp new atlas, it seemed that Lilah was correct. Their course was set for Larien, and nothing would move the rudder to change that. Instead they had to address the crew and explain that the Ship was a living thing, and that it wanted to go to Larien and see if there were unicorns there.

Most of the crew was not happy about this, but some of them seemed deeply moved by it. They seemed to feel that if they were on this magical, living Ship, that meant the Ship had chosen them, specially, for this journey.

"We should probably encourage this idea," Queen Celina said later, in the privacy of the main cabin. "If more of the crew would believe it, I would worry less about there being a mutiny."

"I think we should encourage it because it's true," Celie said. When they all looked at her, she shrugged one shoulder. "If the Ship didn't want them on board, it would probably just toss them into the water. It doesn't need them. So if they're still here, it's because the Ship *has* chosen them."

"See, Cel," Rolf said. "This is why we always ask you what the Castle wants, and now we're asking you what the Ship wants. None of us ever think of these things."

"Even you?" Celie asked him. "You're the next King Glower!"

Celie used to be pleased when her family turned to her with their questions about the Castle and acknowledged her as its favorite, but lately she'd started to wonder. Why was Rolf the heir if she was the Castle's favorite? It was something that she hardly dared think about. She didn't think she'd like to be Queen Glower, and there never had been one. But why? Was it just because the crown only fit on a man's head? That seemed like a stupid reason. And they'd only had the real crown, the Builder's crown, and his rings, for a few months. They could just as easily have made a woman's crown years ago.

"Yes, but I'm the next King Glower because the Castle *likes* me—it doesn't *love* me," Rolf said, as though he'd reasoned this out long ago. "Being king is a horrible job, full of paperwork and people coming to the Castle every week to complain about their neighbor's goats and the fight Pogue started—"

"Hey!" Pogue interrupted. "I haven't started a fight in *months*."

"Very true," Rolf said, shaking his head. "I almost don't recognize you anymore."

Pogue gave Rolf a look that clearly said he'd *like* to start his first fight in months.

"Anyway," Rolf went on breezily, "the Castle gives *you* all the fun jobs, Cel. Raising griffins. Finding lost ship bits. That's because it loves you. It just wants me to be its slave."

"What an interesting way to look at kingship," Queen Celina said in a dry voice. "And not entirely wrong. But we should probably discuss that later. For now we need to talk about what provisions we have, and what we'll do if the Ship won't let us veer course to get more."

"Oh," Lilah said. This was apparently just dawning on her. "Surely if we run out of food, the Ship will help us get more."

But she didn't sound sure. The Castle couldn't make food, and so it stood to reason that the Ship couldn't, either.

"If we continue on this same course, we'll go right by the Neira Isles," Orlath said in Grathian, using a brass ruler and a soft pencil to draw a line from their current position to a group of islands to the southwest. "There's a fine port here on the largest island where we can resupply." He drew a circle around a small dot on a heart-shaped island and frowned. "If the Ship doesn't slow down as we go past, we might try to signal to some of their ships to bring us provisions. They could pull alongside, perhaps."

"Or we could use the griffins," Celie replied in the same language.

"The very thing!" Lulath said. "We can fly with the griffins to the port and back to pick up the supplies we need."

They all stopped to think about this. Slowly they began to nod, and the mood started to lift.

"Dagger could make the flight, if he flew with you and Rufus," Rolf admitted in Sleynth. "I don't think he could carry me. Certainly not me and supplies. But some light things. Loaves of bread?"

Celie knew how much it took Rolf to say that, and she rubbed his back. It was hard to be separated from your griffin, and to offer to let him fly over the ocean to a strange port . . . that would be very hard indeed.

"He's coming along nicely in his training," Pogue said. "He'll stay with Rufus and Arrow, and we should be able to sling some light things across his back."

"And I'll send Lady Griffin without a rider as well," Queen Celina said. "Mainly because I don't think anyone's ever ridden her!"

"That settles that," Orlath said in Grathian. He didn't look happy, though. "With the exception of one, rather large, problem."

"What's that?" Lilah asked.

"Water," Orlath told her. "We'll need to refill our barrels of fresh water—more urgently than we need bread. But I don't think the griffins can carry a full water barrel, marvelous as they are."

"But we don't know that the Ship won't stop and let us get supplies," Lilah pointed out brightly. "If it really wants us to go all the way to Larien, surely it will turn into the port of its own accord?" She looked around the cabin, waiting for an answer that didn't come.

"I'm not concerned about the water," Queen Celina said. They all turned to her in confusion. She was smiling. "It will give me a chance to show off," she told them. "Magic has its limits, as do I, not being a full wizard. So I can't make food—at least, not food that will taste good enough to eat." She made a face. "But I can, in fact, make seawater into freshwater." She tilted her head to one side, and a broad smile stretched across her face. "In fact, I've been told I have quite the gift for it!"

"O my new mother!" Lulath exclaimed, reaching across the atlas to clasp both her hands. "A radiant queen, and yet a wizard of such power!"

"Can you really?" Rolf asked in awe. "That's amazing! That's probably the most useful kind of spell you could do!" He also reached over and gave their mother's arm a pat. "I don't think even Bran can do something like that!"

Queen Celina squeezed Lulath's hands in return and then released them to wave casually, as though this announcement were of little note. "Oh, I'm sure he can," she said lightly. "It's really quite simple."

But Celie could tell that her mother was proud of herself, and rightly so. Lilah was near tears of joy now, as well.

"It's really going to happen," she whispered. "We're going to make it. We're going to find the unicorns."

Lulath hugged her. Even Celie hugged her. Excitement was rising in all of them. They were going on an adventure, in a living Ship. They would have freshwater. They would have fresh food. All they needed to worry about was finding unicorns.

Unicorns!

That, and the griffins trying to eat the unicorns, as Rolf pointed out later.

"Do you really think they will?" Celie asked. They were sitting in the bow of the Ship, looking out over the ocean. It was beautiful, and somewhat terrifying. They had already lost sight of Grath, and though in the distance they could see a few other ships, there was a great deal of sky and a great deal of water. And nothing else.

Celie pointed to where Lorcan was lying sprawled in the sun. Lulath's girls were curled around him or on him, napping. Dagger, who was at Rolf's feet, noticed the pile of creatures and went over to join them, flopping down on top of Nisi. Rolf leaped up to rescue the small black-and-white dog, but she wriggled her way out from under Dagger and put her head on his foreleg without even appearing to wake up.

"See?" Celie said.

"Well, yes," Rolf said. "And it's not like they've eaten all the sheep at the Castle, or anything like that. Which makes me wonder why they attacked the unicorns. Are they natural enemies, like pigs and thornsnakes, or something?"

"Or is there something horrible about the unicorns that we should know?" Celie said, picking up his line of thought.

Then they both laughed, because it was ludicrous to think that unicorns could be horrible in any way.

Chapter 13

Two weeks later they could see the green humps of the Neira Isles. And not a moment too soon. They were running low on food, though the queen had regularly replenished the water barrels, so there was freshwater aplenty. The cook had used this water to stretch the food supplies by making everything into a soup. The sailors had also taught Rolf and Pogue how to drag a net alongside the ship to catch fresh fish, but Queen Celina was insisting that they needed flour and eggs and fruit.

But the Ship showed no signs of slowing.

In fact, as the largest island grew clearer, the Ship veered course to give it a wide berth.

"We're not going to stop," Lilah said.

They were gathered around the useless wheel. Orlath stood with one hand on it often, and when he wasn't touching it he had a loop of rope tied around it, as though fixing their course. He had told them it was to put the crew at ease, so they wouldn't realize how much the Ship was doing on its own, but he had confessed to Celie and Lilah that it made him feel safer as well. It was also a good vantage point to see what needed to be done: the Ship steered itself, but now it left the sails and rigging to the sailors, and in that Orlath was still needed to give orders.

"We'll have to ready the griffins to fly," Queen Celina said, her brows pulled together with worry. "I wish I could go myself, but I'd have to ride double, and then that griffin wouldn't be able to carry as much back."

"It is being perhaps better that you are going, or I," Orlath said in Sleynth.

Queen Celina shook her head. "As nervous as it makes me to send my children to a strange country alone, I think it's best if we don't overburden the griffins. It's quite a distance for them to fly, even without carrying the supplies."

"So, you think that Celie, Pogue, Lulath, and I had better go?" Lilah asked.

"And me," Rolf said. "I'll go double with Celie, and then Dagger—"

Queen Celina put a gentle hand on his arm. "Rolf, I've thought about this a great deal. Dagger is far too young. Even without a rider it will tire him too much. There's no sense in his going, and no sense in burdening one of the griffins with two riders. You and I will stay and try to be patient." She smiled at her son as though she knew he wouldn't like what she'd said.

"It's the best way to do it," Lilah said. "No griffin carrying double, and all of them at least half-grown."

"Now the trick is going to be how fast we can get to port, buy what we need to buy, and get back," Pogue said. He looked at the ocean streaming by on either side of the Ship. "We're moving pretty fast."

"With that I am helping," Orlath said. "When an hour comes, I will be curling of sails and dropping of anchors, that the great speed of this great Ship is slowed."

"We can only be hoping this noble Ship does not have objections," Lulath said, running his fingers through his hair.

The steady supply of freshwater meant that they were able to wash and keep their clothing clean, but they all had only one set of clothes, and it was odd to see Lulath in the same coat day after day. Celie herself was beginning to hate her green gown, and wished that she were as tall as Lilah and Queen Celina. They were of a similar size, and had swapped gowns a few days ago for the sake of variety.

"I'll speak to the Ship," Lilah declared.

She marched down the stairs from the helm to the main deck, then up the stairs to the foredeck. At first they all stood there watching her in mystification, but when she leaned over the rail in the bow, Celie and Lulath both started to run. They caught up to Lilah just as she put her stomach on the rail and leaned over as far as she could.

Celie immediately grabbed the back of Lilah's skirts, and Lulath put himself on the rail alongside her, with one long arm over her back. Together, Lilah and Lulath leaned down toward the figurehead, and Lilah began to shout.

"We need to slow down!" Lilah called. "You've got to let us slow down! We have to get supplies from Neira, all right? Or we'll all die!"

They waited, but nothing happened. Celie pulled Lilah back onto her feet, and Lulath straightened with a groan. The blood had rushed to both of their heads.

"Was that being helping?" Orlath came up behind them. He was nervously stroking Jocko, who looked ready to leap at the figurehead himself, to join the game.

"I guess we'll find out when we try to slow down," Lilah said.

"Shall I begin?" Orlath asked.

"Of a sureness," Lulath said.

Orlath strode to the end of the foredeck and cupped his hands to his mouth. He rapidly gave orders, and men began to race around, pulling in the sails and tying them fast. Two of the men went below to lower the enormous anchor.

Lilah leaned back against the bow rail. She took Lulath's hand in one of hers, Celie's in the other. Rufus, sensing their tension, came to lean against Celie, and then Lorcan and Juliet, not to be outdone, had to lean against their people. The weight of the griffins nearly knocked them all over the rail.

The sails were furled. The anchor hit the water with a splash. The Ship's breakneck speed began to slow.

Lulath reached across and grabbed Celie's other hand so that they made a circle. The griffins were forced to stand under their arms, and Lulath, Celie, and Lilah all cheered. And then Lilah solemnly thanked the Ship.

"We'd better get ready," Lilah said.

"We don't really have any riding clothes to change into," Celie said, letting go of their hands and feeling self-conscious as Pogue and Rolf came toward them.

"No, of course not, but we'll need to make a list of what we'll want and how much, and collect some money." She froze.

"Do we have any money?" Celie asked, knowing exactly what her sister had just realized.

"I never have any," Rolf said, wide-eyed.

"I have a few Grathian coins," Pogue said. "But I don't think it will be enough."

"Here's the purse," Queen Celina said, gliding up to them. She handed Lulath a fat leather purse that chinked reassuringly. "Why don't you carry it, Lulath, darling? And Lilah, let's trade gowns again. I'm very fond of the one you're wearing."

Pogue went to talk to the cook about what supplies they would need, while Lulath stowed the purse deep in his coat and began to adjust all the griffins' harnesses. Celie followed her mother and Lilah to the cabin she and Lilah shared.

"Where did that purse come from?" Celie asked her mother after the door had been latched. The cabin wasn't large, so she had to sit on Lilah's bottom bunk and draw her legs up while her mother undid the laces at the back of Lilah's gown. "I've never seen it before."

"You've just never noticed it before," her mother corrected her. "And why would you have?" She helped Lilah out of the gown and laid it on the top bunk while Lilah undid her laces.

"Is the money Grathian or Sleynth?" Celie asked. "And what happens if they don't like Grathian money— or Sleynth!—on Neira?"

"It's perfectly good gold, and some silver," her mother said. "And they're a trading post. There's no reason why they wouldn't take it. None at all."

"Thank heavens you had it," Lilah said. "I never carry any money! I don't think I've even seen Grathian money!" She laughed as she slipped her own gown over her head.

"Money is money," their mother retorted. She yanked at Lilah's laces, making her oldest daughter yelp. "Neither of you need to worry about it."

"Fine," Lilah wheezed. "But I need to breathe to ride Juliet!"

"I'm sorry, Lilah, darling," Queen Celina said, contrite.

She helped Lilah adjust the gown, and then she braided Celie's hair so that it would stay out of her way. The sisters helped their mother into her gown, and they all went to the main deck together.

The tide was still drawing them forward, toward the mouth of NeiMai Harbor, as Orlath told them it was called, though if the Ship didn't turn, they would pass right by it. The island was shaped like a large crescent, and NeiMai Harbor contained the only real city on all three islands. They could not only see it but also see a fleet of fishing boats scattered about the ocean ahead of them.

"Will the fishermen help us if we need it?" Celie asked Orlath.

"Of course," Orlath said. Then he switched to Grathian so that he could speak more easily. "The main business here is fishing, but they also resupply ships passing by. They would lose a large part of their income if word got out that they had failed to aid a party of distressed travelers."

He paused. "But even as slow as we're going now," he added, "we go much faster than any other ship I've captained, let alone a fishing boat. If the Ship chooses to speed up again, there's no prayer another ship could catch it. The griffins are the only hope for that." Seeing Celie's concern, he patted her shoulder. "But I see no reason to worry about it now."

Celie frowned, not reassured.

"Oh, come on, Cel!" Rolf chided her. "What are the odds that the Ship won't let you catch back up? It could have dumped all of us long ago, if it really wanted to go to Larien on its own!"

"All right, all right, I know," she said, mollified.

They said their good-byes and then climbed onto the backs of the griffins. Dagger was keen to join them, so Rolf had to keep both hands on his harness to stop him from leaping off the rail. Lulath's girls tried to climb up Lorcan and get in the baskets slung from his harness, so Queen Celina put one under each arm, and Orlath did the same, much to the disgust of his monkey, which climbed into the rigging, muttering to itself in protest.

"We're not as close as we could be," Orlath said. "But if you leave now, by the time you're done bartering, we won't be just a speck on the horizon, either."

And on that cheery note, they lined up their griffins and pointed them toward the harbor, and the griffins surged into the air. Down below them on the deck, Dagger screamed with frustration, and the girls began to bark.

It was glorious to be flying again, and such a distance. They'd flown a great deal of the way from Sleyne to Grath, but since arriving at the Sanctuary most flights had been loops over the gardens or short jaunts down to the shipyard. It was terrifying to fly over the open sea, but also very exhilarating.

Celie had never fallen off Rufus before—not while he was flying, anyway. And she could swim, though she'd never been in the ocean before. So she clung to the harness tightly, but held her head high and let the wind whip her hair back and bring tears to her eyes. She looked over at Lilah and saw that her sister was grinning, and so were Pogue and Lulath.

Pogue called something to Arrow, and Arrow dove down until his talons dragged in the waves, then soared back up again. Pogue let out a cheer. Then they all joined in, skimming the tops of the waves and rising back up again, hooting.

Celie loosened her grip on the harness, and even took one hand off to wave at the fishing boats they began to pass. The fishermen all stopped, nets trailing from their hands, and stared. A few waved, but most just stood with their mouths open. One man lost his grip on the net and it drifted into the water. The other fishermen on that boat began to shout and wave their arms, berating the hapless man who had lost the net.

Without even needing a signal, Rufus dove after the net. He had to put all four legs right into the water, which also splashed Celie, soaking her skirt and shoes, but he managed to snag the net with three of his four claws. Wings flapping, he struggled to raise it out of the water, however, and Celie realized that it was full of fish.

"Pogue," she called.

Pogue and Arrow were there immediately, and so were Lulath and Lorcan. They all swooped in and grabbed some of the net, hauling it up out of the water and over the narrow deck of the low fishing boat.

"Drop it," Celie called, much as she would have for a ball during a game of catch, and the griffins obliged.

With a sound between a thump and a splat, the laden net landed on the deck. Long blue fish began to flop and writhe everywhere. The men cheered, and then set to work scooping the catch into baskets.

Celie gave them a jaunty salute, and they continued on to the harbor.

Chapter
14

⌒≈⌒

NeiMai Harbor was not as busy or as large as the harbor
in Grath, but it was a lot more fascinating.

For one thing, the harbor had been divided right down
the middle. On the left side, the docks were for the fishing
fleet, and past the docks were sets of scales and baskets
and things clearly meant to weigh, measure, and market
the fish. On the right side were the larger docks for the
enormous merchant ships, and beyond them were a series
of booths containing all manner of supplies. There was a
great pyramid of water barrels, and other smaller barrels
that held things like flour, salted meat, and beer.

The Neirans all wore clothing in shades of blue that
reminded Celie of the sea. Both men and women wore
long, straight skirts that seemed to be just large rectangles
of cloth wrapped around and around the waist and held
up with a belt. The women wore sleeveless bodices and

necklaces of red and orange beads, while the men wore nothing above the waist but the same beads.

They landed on an empty length of dock on the right side, near a large Grathian ship called the *Dragon of the Sea*. Everywhere sailors and merchants alike stopped what they were doing to gawk at them, and Celie wished her mother had come after all.

But Lulath was a suitable replacement.

He immediately waved to the sailors on the *Dragon of the Sea* and called out in Grathian that he hoped they had had good luck in their trading.

"You will soon be home," he told them. "And all is well there!"

"How do you know they're returning to Grath?" Celie whispered.

"The flag," he said, pointing. It was the Grathian red-and-gold check with a blue crown in the middle, which hung from a flagpole mounted on the rear of the ship. "It hangs from the aft of the ship on the way home, but the top of the mast on the way out."

"Ah."

A man with close-cropped gray hair and skin browned and roughened by a lifetime on the sea approached them. He had a small board with a sheet of paper attached to it under one arm, and wore an open blue vest with his blue skirt. He bowed to them, and they all bowed back.

"Grathian?" he asked.

"Yes," Lulath said. "I am Prince Lulath of Grath, and this is my betrothed, Princess Delilah of Sleyne; her sister, Princess Cecelia of Sleyne; and the good knight of Sleyne, Sir Pogue."

The man went pale beneath his tan. "It's true," he said, almost as though he were speaking to himself. "Griffins!"

"Yes, good sir," Lulath said politely. "And they are griffins in dire need of supplies, if we are to get where we are going!"

"They flew so far?" The man began to slowly walk around the group. "From Grath?" He raised his shaggy eyebrows.

"Only from our Ship," Celie said politely. "But the Ship will not stop, even for supplies; it's . . . eager to stay on course."

He gave a baffled look, but then his eyes were drawn back to the griffins. But if he was this astonished by the animals, she really didn't want to overset his brain by explaining the truth about their Ship.

"Are you the harbormaster?" Lulath asked, distracting him.

"What?" He blinked, then looked down at his writing materials as though he'd never seen them before. "Yes, yes, I am."

He licked his upper lip, then produced a pencil from behind his ear and began to scratch something on the paper. Their names, presumably. This was confirmed when he asked Celie and Pogue to spell their names for him. Celie was ready to translate for Pogue, but he immediately supplied the information, even pronouncing the letters in the Grathian way. Lulath beamed at him.

"My brother Orlath is a fine teacher, is he not?" Lulath asked, and Pogue just nodded.

"Purpose of visit?"

"To supply our Ship," Lulath said. He produced both the purse and a scrap of paper with their shopping list on it.

"Very well," the man said. Then he paused and looked at the griffins again, and an expression of mild panic came into his eyes. "Are you going to tie those beasts here?" he asked.

"No, no," Lulath assured him. "They will stay with us."

"Ah, that seems wise," he said. He licked his lip again. "Do they, can they . . . how will they carry the water?"

"We are not in need of water," Lulath said. "We have plenty."

This made the man gape as much as when he'd first seen the griffins. Freshwater at sea was more precious than gold, and infinitely more useful. Celie was willing to bet they'd never had someone come to NeiMai whose first item of business wasn't getting their water barrels refilled.

"Very good," the harbormaster said, and he finally stepped aside. "Welcome to NeiMai."

They all thanked him and strolled past with their hands on their griffins' backs. Some of the bustle and talk had come back to the marketplace, but it was somewhat stilted, and Celie was convinced that most of the talk was about them.

"I didn't know you spoke Grathian so well," Lilah said to Pogue as they approached a miller's stall.

"Well, I wanted to finally understand what Lulath was saying," he joked.

Lilah looked offended, but Celie and Lulath burst out laughing.

"Time for this haggling," Lulath said in Sleynth. "I am not finding myself good for such things, but will bravely try!"

"Allow me," Lilah said sweetly.

She stepped up to the plank table in front of a giant pyramid of flour barrels. Celie held her breath. Lilah was very good at finding bargains when it came to clothing, but *flour*? And her Grathian was not as good as Celie's. She got ready to intervene on her sister's behalf.

"Good day to you," Lilah said, and her accent was not too bad. "We are in need of four barrels of flour."

"Good day to being with you, gentlewoman," the miller replied. His accent was slightly worse than Lilah's, which was reassuring. "What bold creatures you bring!"

"Thank you," Lilah said. "They are very dear to us. And they love cakes." She nodded at the barrels. "We are short on time."

"I understand," the man said. He signaled to an apprentice to roll out some of the barrels. "That will be two gold, Grathian or Neiran, please, gentlewoman."

Pogue made a choking noise. "Is that normal here?" he whispered to Lulath in Sleynth.

Celie realized the other drawback to having Lilah negotiate: Lilah had never bought flour or sugar or eggs in her life. Lulath and Pogue would have to tell her if she was making a bad bargain. And Celie just hoped Lilah would listen and not get stubborn.

"It is the robbing of babes," Lulath said in Sleynth. He stepped forward.

"Thievery," Lilah said loudly in Grathian. "And I am *not* this gentlewoman you say—I am a princess!" She sighed as though she'd never been so disappointed in her life. "We need flour. For our royal party. And the griffins. I'd thought to get it here, but someone else must have flour." She began to look around.

The man gave her a shrewd look. He might or might not believe she was a princess, but he clearly respected her ploy.

"One gold, twelve silver," he said. "Because I would hate for griffins to hunger." He leaned over the counter to have a look at the animals.

"One gold," Lilah said. "Oh, look." She pointed off to the left. "Someone sells flour right there! A nice fat man," she added. "His flour makes very good cakes indeed!"

Pogue made a sound that was probably a laugh, but he managed to turn it into a sneeze. Celie just marveled at her sister. The miller they were dealing with looked like he'd been sucking lemons.

"One gold, two silver," he said.

"Hmmm." Lilah drummed her fingers on the plank. She was still studying the other merchant. "Do his casks look fuller to you?" she asked Celie. "I hate to be *cheated*."

"One. Gold."

"Done," Lilah said crisply.

Lulath put a fat gold coin down on the table. The man swept it into a pocket without looking at it while his boy rolled the four barrels around to them. Pogue and Lulath got to work figuring out how to hang the barrels from the griffins' harnesses. They finally settled on putting one on each side of Lorcan and one on each side of Arrow, but agreed that they would move them around so that there was just one barrel on each griffin once they had something to act as a counterweight.

"Can I?" the miller said, right in Celie's ear.

She jumped, and Rufus squawked. The man leaped backward as well, then started to edge back around the plank.

"Can you what?" Celie asked when she recovered.

"Can I touch one?" the man said in a rush.

"Oh," Celie said, blinking. "Of course!"

He crept back and held out one hand to Rufus. Rufus sniffed it, then swiped his head over the man's palm. The man let out a surprisingly youthful giggle.

"So soft," he exclaimed.

"Yes," Celie said with pride. "They're lovely, aren't they?"

She and the man shared a smile, and then they moved on to the next booth, where Lilah managed to get them a barrel of salted pork, and then one of salted beef, for a price that Lulath assured her was thievery on *their* part.

They started to gather a crowd, mostly of children who wanted a closer look at the griffins. Some of them also dared to come up and touch. The griffins bore it stoically, much as they bore the weight of the goods being tied to them. This made Celie even more glad they hadn't brought Dagger: he would have snapped at anyone who tugged at his wings the way a small girl had just tugged at Lorcan's, but Lorcan just gave her a look that made her back away. Then she grinned and ran off to whisper with her friends, undaunted.

"I do wish we'd brought Lady Griffin," Celie fretted as they went to the final stop, a stall that sold fine blue and gray fabric. "I think this is getting too heavy."

"I wish there was a way we could signal," Pogue said. He shielded his eyes and looked out beyond the harbor. "Do you think a ship could carry us some of the way out?" He poked Celie in the shoulder with his other hand. "Do you see that?"

"No, what?" she asked in dread, also looking.

The sun was beating down on them, but the afternoon was turning toward evening, and Celie was starting to feel anxious. How far away was the Ship now?

"Here," Pogue said. He bent down and put his arms around Celie's legs so that he could hold her up high. "Look southeast."

It made her feel odd to be held like this. He had her hoisted almost up to his shoulder, with his cheek against her hip. She tried to concentrate on what he'd seen. It wasn't hard, though, once she saw it.

"Celie, what are you doing?" Lilah asked in shock when she turned around with several bolts of cloth in her arms. "Pogue Parry, you put her down!"

"All right, let me down," Celie said to Pogue. "But one of us should stand on a barrel and wave."

"What are you talking about?" Lilah demanded.

"Lady Griffin," Celie said. "She's on her way across the harbor!"

"Well, praise be," Lilah said. "I think poor Juliet is going to fall over!"

They moved to the seawall where Lady Griffin could clearly see them and began to unload the other griffins. Celie hopped up on the wall and waved both her arms until she was sure that the griffin queen was heading directly toward her.

Some of the fishermen coming in to dock waved exuberantly back at first, sure that she was signaling them.

Celie felt like an idiot, trying to point and signal that it was nothing to do with them. Finally Lilah told her she was just making things worse.

Lady Griffin, who had been asleep in Queen Celina's cabin when they'd left, preened herself and accepted their gratitude as if it were merely her due. They were almost afraid to suggest putting the cargo on her, but she gazed into the distance and stood very still while they tried, and they set to redistributing the goods with great cheer.

Since Lady Griffin didn't have a rider, they were able to get all four flour barrels on her harness, plus strap the fabric across her back. Then Lulath managed to balance a large basket of bright orange fruits on top of that.

"You're wonderful," Celie told her again.

She fed Lady Griffin one of the spiky green fruits that a couple of the children had given them. The griffins adored it, but Celie and the others were afraid to eat it. The spikes didn't seem to bother griffin beaks, but Celie thought they looked too sharp to put in a human mouth.

"Lady? Gentleman?" It was the other miller, the round one they hadn't bought their flour from. The harbormaster was hovering at his side . . . well, slightly behind him.

"Yes?" Lulath looked up from testing the balance of the salt pork on Lorcan's shoulder. "What can we help you fine gentlemen with?"

They'd been tying the large things in front of the wings, right alongside each griffin's neck, which seemed to be working. They'd see once they got in the air, though. Assuming they could fly at all.

"You have five griffins?" the rotund man asked.

"Yes," Lulath said. He gestured to them all. "Fine beasts, and loyal."

"Of that we have no doubt," the miller said with a smile.

Celie didn't like his smile. Neither did Rufus, who clumsily moved in front of her. The small cask of honey at his side smacked into something else, and she tightened the cord around it to make it more secure.

"And you paid the tax?"

"The tax?" Lulath frowned. He looked past the man to the harbormaster. "Was there a tax, sir? You did not say!" He reached into his coat for the purse, now much lighter, but thankfully not empty.

"Well," the harbormaster said when the other man prodded him forward. "It's to pay for the docking of a ship, and you don't have a ship to dock."

"True," Lulath said. "But if there is a toll of some kind, please allow us to pay it."

"Something's wrong here," Lilah said in Sleynth, in a light singsong. She had a smile fixed on her face, but it was her royal smile, the one used for boring parties with boorish guests.

They all waited. Pogue put a hand to his hip, but he wasn't armed. Instead he moved between Lilah and Celie, his fists ready.

"We want . . . We would consider . . . ," the harbormaster said. He stopped and licked his lips and then looked to the miller for guidance. "Lord Mayor?"

"A griffin," the miller, who was also the mayor, apparently, said. "You have five. We have none. It seems a fair trade. We will take one of your griffins."

Chapter
15

Trade?" Lilah squawked, and Juliet moved restlessly beside her. "Why do we need to trade anything with you? We've spent our good gold and silver here at your port. Why would we need to give you a griffin, too?"

"Now, fair gentlewoman," the mayor began, but Lilah cut him off.

"Your Royal Highness," she said. "I am *Princess* Delilah." She arched an eyebrow. "Think how few ships will come, bringing gold, when they find the princes and princesses of Sleyne and Grath were treated so."

"Think how many will come to see our griffin," the mayor countered. "And think how badly they will look on both your countries when they learn that you paid in false coinage."

He threw down a handful of coins. They jangled on the stones of the quay, and everyone gasped. Celie squatted down to look at them, confused, and behind her she heard Pogue mutter something in Sleynth.

"What?" she asked over her shoulder, touching a coin lightly with a finger.

"That's what I was afraid of," he said, only slightly louder.

"What did you do?" Lilah hissed, bending down to pick up one of the coins to get a closer look at it.

"Me?" Pogue said in a low, intense voice. *"I'm not the wizard!"*

"Mummy *made* this?" Celie yelped. "Can she do that?"

"This is being not the ideal," Lulath whispered.

He stooped to pick up a coin, and then nearly dropped it in surprise.

"Oh," Celie said, getting a good look at one at the same time. "It's Bendeswean."

And it was . . . though just slightly off. Still, it looked and felt very real. Celie bit the coin gently, and then looked at the miller as though confused.

"What is wrong with this?" she asked him loudly. "Haven't you ever seen Bendeswean coins before?" She laughed a little, a fake, brittle sound. "You scared us nearly to death! We thought someone had changed our coins with fakes."

"Bendeswean?" The mayor turned the unfamiliar word around in his mouth. "What is that?"

"Bendeswe is a country to the north," Lilah said acidly. "We passed through it on the way to Grath, which is why our money is Bendeswean." She sighed heavily. "And now we will ignore your accusing, as well as your demand of a griffin."

"The accusations, yes," the mayor said, but he still eyed the coins suspiciously as Lulath handed them back to him. "But not the demand.

"Yai!"

At his shout, a knot of men holding a fishing net burst out of the crowd. They threw the net over Juliet, who was nearest to them. Celie just froze in horror, but luckily Pogue did not.

"Stand hard," he shouted, as they had practiced.

All the griffins, despite their burdens, went into fighting stance. Even Lady Griffin, who hadn't had the lessons at all, raised one talon and lifted her wings. They made a circle around Juliet, who was screaming and biting at the net. One of the men tried to drag the net away, and Pogue took one long stride in front of Lilah and laid the man flat with a punch to the jaw.

Celie recovered her wits and gave the command for the griffins to move forward, pushing the crowd back. Pogue had his dagger out now and was sawing through the net. The miller took a step forward, and Celie snapped her fingers at Lady Griffin.

"Get him," she said.

If there was a specific command for that, Lady Griffin didn't know it. It didn't matter, though. The queen of the griffins understood.

With a battle cry that even someone who had never seen a griffin before could not mistake, Lady Griffin leaped forward. Despite her burdens she reared up on her hind legs and raked the air with her eagle-like front legs. Then her enormous wings snapped out, knocking the closest people in the crowd flat.

The mayor collapsed with a cry, blood seeping from slashes across the front of his chest. A quick glance told Celie they weren't deep, so she didn't bother herself about them. She guessed that they were meant as more of a warning.

"Be glad her mate isn't here," Celie snapped at him. "He eats men like you for dinner!"

"I will have one," the mayor screamed. "Another monster will not get away from me!"

"Quickly," shouted someone behind them.

A trio of fishermen swarmed over the seawall, knives in hand. Celie prepared to send the griffins at them, but they used their thick-bladed knives to hack through the net and free Juliet. One of them saluted Celie and pointed over the wall, and she recognized the man whose net they had rescued.

"Follow them," Lilah screamed, and she urged Juliet over the wall.

Lulath leaped over and then caught Lilah as she jumped. Pogue grabbed Celie around the waist and slung her over, nearly dropping her right on top of Rufus, who had needed no special command to follow Juliet and

Lorcan. Pogue leaped down with Arrow and an apology for Celie, and then Lady Griffin came sailing over the wall and landed neatly in the bow.

Their rescuers came right after, and the rowers began pulling the moment the rescuers' feet hit the deck. One of the men raised the triangular sail as well, and they made it out of the harbor at a steady clip, despite the weight of the extra people, the griffins, and their cargo.

"Please do think not badly of our people, lords and ladies," the oldest of the men said. His Grathian was formal and a little stilted, but clear nonetheless. He laid a hand on the man who had dropped the net, and Celie could see that this was likely his son. "The mayor's father was the best mayor. His son is not a good man, but out of love for the father we gave him the office." He grimaced.

"What did he mean?" Lilah asked, looking over Juliet for injuries. "He said 'Another monster will not get away from me.'"

"Ah, yes," the fisherman said. "Years ago a ship came from the south bearing a strange beast. Like a horse but with a great horn on its head."

"A unicorn!" Lilah exclaimed, straightening.

"Yes, that is how it is called," the man said. "I saw it, poor beast. It must have been wondrous once, but it was aged and in the lowest health." His grip tightened on his son's shoulder. "The mayor made an offer for it, but they refused. He craved an exotic beast to display and raise his

135

status. The people who had brought it said that it was not for sale. They were making for Grath, and beyond, to see if any could cure it. But it died before they left, while they were still fighting with the mayor."

Lilah let out a cry of distress, and Lulath put his arm around her. The fisherman smiled sadly at them.

"Did you also seek the unicorns, to match with your fierce flying beasts?" he asked her.

"Yes," Celie said, because Lilah looked close to tears. "Not because we want to . . . display them," she hurried to say. "But because we come from their true home, and we want to take them back there. They are from a country called Sleyne, like us."

He nodded, and then he took his hand from his son to pat her shoulder. "I'm very sorry, then. That was the last one, and it died here in NeiMai."

Now Lilah was crying for sure, and Celie felt like it, too. What was the point of going to Larien now? Maybe that wasn't even where the Ship was taking them. Or maybe it didn't know, and it thought it would bring back a hold full of unicorns.

"Where is your ship?" the young man who had dropped the net inquired.

They scanned the horizon and saw it, to the south but not too far.

"Can your beasts fly there?"

"We are hoping they can," Lulath said. "Though they are greatly burdened. Thank you for your help." He looked back the way they came, but there seemed to be no one in pursuit. "We have caused you a great deal of trouble."

The father made a rude noise. "My family has fished these waters for a thousand generations, when the mayor's people were rooting in the mud with their pigs on DiMai." He saw Celie's confusion. "That is the smallest island, and not a very worthy one." His smile stretched wide. "And today we have helped expose the mayor's greed *and* brought in the largest catch of the season! All because of you!"

This cheered the rest of the tiny boat's crew immensely, and Celie and her people just a little. They fixed the griffins' burdens and made some adjustments so that they could fly to the Ship, and then they climbed on. Celie had to be boosted into place, and her legs stuck straight out on either side of Rufus's head, but the fishermen didn't seem to find this strange. They were clearly too impressed with the griffins to think anything they did was ungainly.

"You've been wonderful," Lilah told them, recovering her manners.

Lulath tried to give them the rest of the purse, but the older man refused.

"Truly, that was twice the fish we normally catch," he told them. "The boat nearly sank!" He laughed in delight. "We would have helped you sooner, but we were busy unloading!"

There was another round of thanks, and then they took their leave. The griffins nearly capsized the boat, leaping heavily off the side, but the men had their oars ready and they recovered.

They flew close to the water again, but because they were loaded so heavily, and not because they were playing. If it were possible to trudge through the air, that is what they were doing. They were all tired and worried and scared, but the good news was that the Ship appeared to be at a near standstill now.

Catching up to it, with their own crew hailing them triumphantly, raised Celie's spirits a little. Rufus was drooping, as were the others, but he managed to fly high enough to just clear the main deck rail and collapse onto the boards.

The crew, used to the griffins by now, didn't hesitate to rush forward and relieve them of their cargo, and JouJou and Nisi went into an ecstasy of barking. Jocko danced around Lady Griffin until she snapped at him, and he ran to the rigging to sulk.

"My darlings," Queen Celina cried, running forward to kiss them all. "We've been so frightened!" She held Celie at arm's length, then kissed her again. She even grabbed hold of Pogue and kissed his cheek. "When Lady Griffin suddenly left, we were certain you were in danger."

"We were," Pogue said grimly. "Your Majesty, they . . ." But then he looked to Lilah to tell the story.

"First of all," Lilah said crossly, "you gave us counterfeit money you *made* with *magic*. I thought we'd be *arrested!*"

"I'm so sorry, my darlings!" Queen Celina looked stricken. "I thought I did a good-enough job! I didn't think they'd know what Bendeswean coins would look like, if I got the details wrong!" She was wringing her hands, which was unsettling to Celie. Her mother rarely lost her composure in such a way. "But what happened? Is it all right?"

"No, it isn't," Lilah went on. "They tried to steal Juliet!" Her voice broke on a sob. "And then we found out that all the unicorns are dead anyway!" She fell into Lulath's arms as their mother and Orlath gasped in horror.

"Hello, you're back," Rolf said, coming onto the main deck from below. "Er, everything all right?"

"No," Lilah sobbed. "It's all awful!"

"Um, I see," Rolf said. "So. Is now a bad time to mention that one of Lulath's dogs just had puppies?"

Chapter
16

The new dog mother was Kitsi, a regal creature the size of a loaf of bread and blessed with a great quantity of caramel, brown, and white hair—which is why no one had noticed that she was going to have puppies. Now she looked noticeably leaner as she reclined with her four babies nursing busily, and Celie wondered how they had missed it.

"Why does it always have to be my bed?" Rolf said ruefully.

Kitsi had chosen Rolf's bunk to expand her family on. Dagger had also hatched from his egg in the middle of Rolf's bed. Lady Griffin carked, and then leaned forward to nuzzle the puppies. Kitsi thumped her plumed tail in response.

"So that's how she got up there," Queen Celina said.

Rolf slept in the top bunk. Lulath's girls were good jumpers, but not *that* good.

"She must have spread the word that your bed was the best place for having babies," Pogue said. He grinned.

"If she doesn't want to move, you can stay in my cabin with me," Queen Celina told Rolf. "Although that means that Pogue will have to take care of the mother and babies on his own until they're ready."

"Griffins, puppies, they're all the same," Pogue said airily.

Lulath had apparently been too overcome with emotion to speak for a moment. Now he leaned against the side of the bunk and carefully encircled the mother and babies with one long arm.

"Such beauties," he murmured to her in Grathian. "Delicate and lovely as their mother!"

Kitsi thumped her tail again.

Celie looked suspiciously at the other dogs. Was JouJou fatter than usual?

Pogue followed her gaze. "Any more puppies, though, and I think I'd rather swim to Larien," he remarked.

"What's the point?" Lilah said brokenly. She had barely glanced at the puppies, and now she slumped on Pogue's bunk. "I'll see if I can't get the Ship to turn around."

"Now, Lilah, darling," Queen Celina said. "There's no need to despair. The Ship knows what it's doing."

"Does it?" she asked, still listless.

"Come on, cheer up," Rolf said. "First of all, no one

has had puppies on *your* blankets." He held up his hands when he saw they were all about to shout at him to be serious. "Sorry, sorry!

"But anyway, the Castle always knows what's going on, even if we don't. That's why it moves things around, so that we foolish humans can find what we need."

"It's true," Celie agreed. "It showed me the Spyglass Tower weeks before we needed it. I couldn't figure out why we'd need some dry biscuits and a Vhervhish grammar, but sure enough, we did!"

"But how could the Ship know what's on Larien?" Lilah protested. "The Castle knows what it knows because it's all happening inside the Castle."

"But how does the Castle know what's going to happen in the future?" Pogue said. "None of us knew that Khelsh was going to try to take over—otherwise he wouldn't have been allowed in the gates!"

"How *does* the Castle know the future?" Rolf said, pulling at his ear. "I never really thought about it in those terms. So do you think it knew Father was still alive because it could see him returning home in the future, or could it sense that Father wasn't dead?"

"How can we possibly know that?" Lilah said crossly. "We can't, that's how. Just like we can't possibly know how powerful the Ship is! Is it as full of magic and . . . all-knowing as the Castle? Or just a tenth of that?"

No one had an answer. Out in the passageway, the griffins began to whine. The cabin was too small for any of them beside Lady Griffin to fit in, not with all the people in it, and it was becoming extremely crowded. Celie's stomach growled loudly, to her embarrassment.

"I suppose it's dinnertime for all of us," Queen Celina said. "I'm sure the cook is happy to have fresh supplies to work with."

Everyone left the cabin except Lilah, Lulath, and Celie. Celie had been about to follow her mother out and scrounge some food before dinner, but Queen Celina raised her eyebrows and jerked her head for her to stay. Celie made a face at her mother, but her mother's eyebrows just went higher, and Celie turned back to the cabin.

In the past few months Celie had been made to chaperone Lilah and Lulath quite a bit, to make sure they didn't spend all their time kissing, and it was her least favorite duty as a younger sister. Did her mother really think they would start kissing *now*? When Lilah was so upset?

"Oh," Celie said aloud.

"Yes, Celie? What is it?" Lulath asked solicitously. He still had one arm around the dogs, while the other hung down so that his hand was on Lilah's shoulder.

"Oh, nothing," she said.

It just occurred to her that she was supposed to stay there with them because Lilah was so upset, and not to keep her from kissing Lulath too much. But she couldn't say that out loud. Not to either of them, anyway.

Instead she lifted the other dogs up onto the top bunk. At first Kitsi tensed, and Celie and Lulath watched carefully, but then she made a friendly sounding yip and allowed the other dogs to sniff her puppies. Then they all lay down around her, cuddling and warming the puppies with their own furry bodies.

Lilah suddenly grasped Celie's hands, scaring her.

"What?" Celie almost shouted, and Kitsi raised her head and growled.

"What does the Ship want?" Lilah whispered. "I thought I knew! I thought it wanted what I wanted: to find unicorns. But does it?"

"I—I don't know," Celie stammered.

"I want you to find out," Lilah said passionately. "I can't do this, Celie. I can't charge into something blindly like this. I have to know where we're going and why."

"How am I supposed to find that out?" Celie appealed to Lulath.

"If anyone can be finding such a thing, it is being you," Lulath said to her.

He turned to comfort Lilah, and Celie wandered out of the cabin. Pogue was lounging in the passageway outside. He straightened and followed Celie.

"All right?" he asked her.

"No," she said. "I'm not." She realized that she sounded angry, but it wasn't Pogue's fault. She slowed down a little and looked up at him. "Did you hear that?"

"Yes."

"What do you think?"

"I'm angry," Pogue said.

Celie stopped in her tracks to look at him. They were at the bottom of the stairs that led up to the main deck. The light spilling down showed that his jaw was clenched, and his eyes were hard. Celie drew back a little, and he softened.

"I'm not angry *at* you," he said quickly. "I'm angry that your family always does this *to* you. Whenever there's a problem with the Castle—and now the Ship—they look to you for the answer, but the rest of the time they treat you like a child."

Celie couldn't believe it. Someone finally understood! She wanted to hug Pogue, but she put her hands behind her back instead.

"But the Castle loves me best," she said, and it sounded feeble in her own ears.

"That doesn't mean you have to save everyone every time. The worst part is when you do have the answer and they won't listen to you, because you're the youngest."

She put her hands on her face. "I thought no one noticed that but me," she said.

"It's just the same as everyone assuming I would be a blacksmith, without even asking me," Pogue told her. "That's why I noticed."

She nodded. They'd talked about this before.

"Even when I was knighted, it was just . . . it was like it was a game. My family treated it like a passing fancy, like the next morning I'd be back in the forge, and my knighthood would be gone." He drew in a deep breath. "But at the same time they were different around me. My little sisters . . . they all curtsied to me at breakfast. That's why I moved into rooms at the Castle. It was too strange. They believed that I was a knight and that I was the same old Pogue, all at once."

"And my family treats me like a child and like a sage who can decipher all the Castle's whims at the same time," Celie said.

"Exactly," Pogue said. "It's not easy to be two things at once to your family."

"If they're going to make me solve the problem of the Ship," Celie said, "then they should treat me like an adult." She was aware of how childish that sounded, and blushed.

"Exactly."

"So, what do I do?"

Pogue put his hands in his pockets.

"You don't know, either?" She sagged.

"No," he said ruefully. "But it just feels good to be able to say it aloud to someone."

"There is that," Celie agreed. She sighed. "It looks like I'll be finding out what the Ship wants. Because *I* want to know, too!"

"Well, we all want to know," Pogue said. "And the truth of the matter is that you'll have better luck than anyone else. You're more tuned in to the Ship and the Castle, even though your father is the king and your sister owns the Ship."

"Just promise me one thing," Celie said, her heart pounding a little, though she wasn't sure why.

"Of course."

"Whatever solution I come up with, or whatever I discover, you have to back me up."

"Of course—"

She held up a hand to stop him. "No, seriously, Pogue. Promise me. If I say that the Ship wants us to swim back to Grath, you have to support me in that. If I say we're really going to find unicorns, you have to support me. No matter how crazy it sounds, or how dangerous."

Pogue thought for a moment, then nodded. "I promise. I'll support you. I believe in you," he told her.

A rosy glow started in her toes and spread up her entire body. "Thank you," she choked out, and fled to the bow.

In the bow of the ship, leaning over the rail just above the figurehead, Celie felt the wind snap through her hair. She was tired and hungry and disheveled, but she needed to *think*.

What did the Ship want?

What if all the unicorns were dead?

And what about Pogue? What if he was just humoring her? What if she told him a plan, or something she'd learned, and he laughed? What if he was just trying to get her to confide in him, but as soon as she did, he would carry tales back to Rolf, or worse—her mother?

"Stupid," she said aloud. "You're the one who made him promise!"

She pushed those thoughts aside and made herself think about the Ship instead. Then she decided to talk aloud to the Ship. It always helped her think; maybe it would make the Ship think, too.

"They told us the unicorns are all dead," she said, and she imagined her words going straight into the ears of the griffin figurehead. "The last one died years ago, in NeiMai, where we just were.

"So, where are we going? Are we going to Larien? Are we going to see if any unicorns are left?"

The Ship didn't reply. It just surged on. The wind brought tears to her eyes, much as riding Rufus did. Celie didn't have any frame of reference for how fast a ship could sail, but according to Orlath, this was the fastest one he'd ever sailed on. Now that they were back on board with the sails unfurled and the anchor drawn up, it had picked up speed again. Indeed, Celie thought they were going even faster now.

"What's the hurry?"

"Well, it's dinnertime," Rolf said at her elbow.

Celie nearly fell headfirst off the Ship.

"Whoa!" Rolf grabbed her elbows and pulled her back. "Sorry!"

"Don't sneak up on me!"

"I wasn't trying to," he protested. "But anyway: dinnertime."

Grumbling, Celie followed her brother across the deck to the stairs below.

"So," he said when they were almost there, "you were talking to the Ship?"

"Yes," she muttered.

She couldn't tell if he was making fun of her or not. After her conversation with Pogue, she was still feeling very sensitive about how her family treated her. Maybe she'd been overreacting, but maybe not.

"Did it answer?"

Again, she couldn't decide whether he was poking fun.

"No," she said, curt.

The Ship shivered as they went down the stairs. Celie and Rolf had to clutch at the rope nailed along the wall for a railing to avoid falling down. When they reached the bottom of the stairs, Rolf looked at her.

"What do you think that was?"

"We changed direction," she said.

"Did we?"

Celie nodded. She had always had a keen sense of direction, which was one of the reasons why she never got lost in the Castle. The Ship had been going southeast before.

"We're going due south now," she told Rolf.

Orlath came out of the main cabin, where they ate. "We're going south," he said. His tanned face was pale in the lamplight.

"That's very bad," he told them.

Chapter
17

Celie and her family ended up eating dinner standing on the rear deck next to the Ship's wheel. While they all ate awkwardly, standing up, Orlath used the Ship's instruments to confirm that they were indeed headed south. Not southeast or southwest, but due south.

Pogue and Lulath took turns trying to move the wheel, but it was still stuck fast. The Ship had set a new course, and would not be deterred.

"But what is to the south?" Queen Celina asked. She wrinkled her brow, thinking. "I can think of nothing on the maps. Just more water."

"Larien is southeast," Orlath said. He spoke mostly in Grathian now, and Celie wasn't sure if this was a compliment to how well they'd learned the language, or a sign that he was too upset to try speaking Sleynth. "And if we were to aim the Ship southwest, it is a long distance, but after some months we would arrive in Xath."

"What's that?" Pogue asked.

"A vast and rather hostile continent," he told them. "Xath is where my little Jocko is from. They have many creatures that you have doubtless never heard of, and trees that darken the sky, they reach so far toward the sun. But the people do not take kindly to visitors, and we would run out of supplies long before we reached it."

"But due south?" Queen Celina pressed.

"Due south there is nothing but the Well," Orlath said grimly.

"What well?" the queen asked.

"The *Well*," Orlath said—and by the emphasis Celie could tell that it was capitalized, at least in Orlath's mind—"is a great vortex of water through which no ship can pass."

"The Great Whirlpool?" Rolf said, his eyes wide. "Are you talking about the Great Whirlpool?"

"Oh, the very, no," Lulath whispered.

"A whirlpool?" Pogue asked. "You mean . . . ?" He took his hands off the Ship's wheel, which was holding fast anyway, and described a circle in the air with his hands.

"Exactly, Sir Pogue," Orlath said. "A great swirl of water that sucks down any ship hapless enough to come near it. Most whirlpools are caused by a few rocks, and are easy enough to avoid. They occur at the base of cliffs, usually.

"But the Well, or the Great Whirlpool, is in the middle of the ocean. There are no rocks, no land nearby, nothing that would seem to cause it. It's five times larger than any other known whirlpool, and the waters for miles around draw you in. If you're close enough to see it, you cannot turn back."

"And that's where we're going?" Lilah asked, her horrified expression perfectly mirroring what Celie felt was on her own face. "How soon will we get there?"

Orlath spread out his hands and looked at them. "Two weeks? Three?" he said. "I've never been; only heard tales from those rare survivors—men who jumped from their ships and swam away when the Well had their vessels in its pull. And our Ship is going so much faster than any other ship I've sailed on. What is four weeks for another ship will be three for this one."

"So it's all right to start to panic now?" Rolf said.

"I can't believe the Ship would do this," Lilah said faintly.

"I am believing it not," Lulath said stoutly. "I am believing that there is some planning, some thing in its workings, that we cannot see with our little eyes."

"What *did* you say to the Ship?" Rolf asked Celie.

"What? I—" Celie looked for a place to put her empty plate down. "What do you mean?"

"You were talking to the Ship when I came to fetch you for dinner," Rolf persisted. "What did you say to it?"

Everyone was looking at Celie, who was starting to wish she hadn't scarfed down all that food just now. Was this her fault? Had the Ship decided that it was worthless now that the unicorns were dead? Behind Rolf, Pogue was still standing at the wheel. He gave her an encouraging nod.

"Well," she said. "I just went to the bow to talk to the Ship . . . after Lilah told me to find out what the Ship wanted," she couldn't help adding. "And I was saying to the Ship that we didn't know where we were going, and that someone had told us the unicorns were all dead."

Lilah gasped, but the others all looked thoughtful.

"And then the Ship changed course?" Queen Celina asked, as though it were a magical problem she was solving.

"Not then," Celie said. "When we walked below deck."

"That was only about two minutes later," Rolf pointed out. Then he held up his hands, defensive, as both Pogue and Celie gave him sharp looks. "I'm just trying to make sure we have all the information," he protested.

"You think the Ship is so despondent now that it's trying to . . . destroy itself?" Lilah asked shrilly.

"No," Queen Celina said. "I don't think it thinks that way. But perhaps . . . Hmm."

"Perhaps what?" Rolf asked. "We have to turn this thing around so that we don't die."

Queen Celina tipped her head back and forth. "I'd like to see the atlas, Orlath," she said. "I want you to mark the entire area where the Well might be. And then I want you to mark our course from Grath to this very minute."

"Of course, Your Majesty," he said. He looked at the wheel, then shrugged and said to Pogue, "You can keep trying if you like, but it's probably useless."

Pogue agreed. "I think I'll groom Arrow and get him to bed early," he said. "That was quite a stressful day for the griffins."

"I'd better get to Rufus," Celie agreed.

"No, you don't," Queen Celina said, hooking her arm. "You come with me. I want you to see this, too, so that the next time you talk to the Ship, you have a better idea of what to say."

"I'll groom Rufus," Pogue offered.

Everyone scattered to tackle their various tasks. Celie found herself looking at maps and charts in Orlath's cabin with her mother and Orlath, which she normally would have enjoyed. But right now she couldn't shake the feeling that she was in trouble. At first this made her embarrassed, but then she started to get angry.

"What did I do?" she asked her mother at last. "I just did what Lilah told me to do," she said, answering her own question.

"What are you talking about, darling?" Queen Celina said, looking up with a startled expression.

She was helping Orlath use some cartographer's brass implements to draw a circle around the area that might hold the Well. It was very large.

"Lilah told me to find out where the Ship was going, and what it planned, so I talked to it, it changed course, and now everyone's mad at me. But it's not my fault! I didn't know this would happen!"

"Of course it's not your fault, darling," Queen Celina said. She put down her pencil and stroked Celie's cheek. "No one's mad at you!"

Celie raised her eyebrows.

Orlath put down his ruler. "I shall leave to let you talk about this," he said, and Celie's heart sank, but then he added, "However, I would first like to say that I am not mad, and I don't think anyone else is, either. Lulath's letters are always full of praise for your whole family, and of course, poems to Lilah's beauty, but also full of compliments to your boldness and intelligence, Celie. The moment the Ship left harbor of its own whim, I thought at once, at least Celie is on board!

"We will be well." He squeezed her shoulder and then went out.

"Will we?" Celie said, feeling a little breathless. She was both flattered and concerned now: people really were thinking that she would save them, that she had all the answers.

"No one is angry," her mother said. "They're frightened.

Very frightened." She rubbed her eyes. "I don't think I've slept the night through since we started on this journey.

"We've never known where the Ship was taking us," Queen Celina reminded Celie. "We're only assuming that we're going to Larien, because of Lilah's obsession with unicorns. The Ship may have planned to take us to the Well the entire time. We don't know. It's convenient to say 'Celie to talked the Ship and now we've turned onto a more dangerous course,' but if anyone is blaming you, they're only doing it because they're being foolish, or are simply too terrified to think clearly."

She took Celie's hands in her own. "You've grown up so much in the past two years," she said. "When we came home from that ordeal, being injured and lost, and finding the Castle under siege with you inside it . . . seeing you leap off the wall." Queen Celina shuddered. "Well, I think that's when Daddy and I both realized that you weren't a little girl anymore, and that you really did have a special bond with the Castle. But it's just so hard to reconcile that young woman fighting for her home and her family with that little girl, always dusty and mussed from climbing around old storerooms."

"And finding figureheads for ships in them," Celie reminded her mother, but not because she was angry. She was a little tearful, to be honest.

"That's right. You're always doing something astonishing," Queen Celina said, and hugged her. "But you don't have to solve all our problems, Celie, darling. That's not your job. We'll work this out together."

"Then what *is* my job?" Celie couldn't help but ask. She wanted to be solving their problems. She wanted to be doing *something*.

"To just be Celie," her mother said, giving her another hug. Then she looked at the clock on the wall. "And for right now, to go to bed! I shouldn't have kept you so long."

"But won't you show me more of the maps first?" Celie wheedled.

"Of course, darling," her mother said, shaking her head as though to clear it. "You have such a gift with them. That's why I wanted you to have a look."

Queen Celina showed Celie the map of the vast emptiness they were sailing through. At the top was Grath, and then not very far from Grath on the map was the Neira Isles. It was disheartening to think that they had sailed for two weeks in the very fast Ship to reach islands that were only a couple of inches away. Larien was much, much farther from Neira than Neira was from Grath, and so was the Well, but according to the lines they had just drawn, they were headed straight to the Well. If they began to bear west, however, they would go around the Well and be able to reach Xath eventually.

"The map isn't accurate in regard to Xath," Queen Celina told her. "So few ships sail there that Orlath said the distance may be greater or perhaps closer. It also depends on the course you take to avoid the Well."

"But we might not be able to avoid the Well," Celie pointed out.

"True; for right now we are headed straight toward it. But we do have quite a bit of time to turn in either direction. Apparently most captains prefer to change course immediately after the Neira Isles. Perhaps the Ship knows that it can cut it a little closer."

"Do you think the Ship wants to . . . kill itself? And us, too?"

"Oh, my darling, no!" Queen Celina said, holding Celie close. "I don't think the Ship thinks that way, if it really is doing what we would call 'thinking.' From what I've studied and learned about magic, it's probably a very complicated sort of spell in every material that sort of works together, but I don't know that it can really *think*." Her mother smiled and shook her head.

Celie was almost entirely certain her mother was wrong. The Castle could think. The Castle moved things—rooms, furniture—and it did it with good reason. It had provided a place for Celie and Lilah to hide during Khelsh's awful occupation. It had guided Celie right to Rufus's egg, and helped her keep Rufus a secret until she was ready to show him to everyone. It had waited to get rid of Arkwright until the Glowers had closed all the secret passages built by the Arkish invaders.

The Castle could think.

Which meant the Ship could think, most likely. Which meant there was a very good chance that the Ship was headed straight for the Well, and only it knew why.

There was nothing they could do.

Chapter
18

In the morning there was excellent news: a Grathian ship had been sighted. It was coming from the southeast—from Larien, most likely. Orlath had someone in the crow's nest signaling with small flags by the time Celie was up and dressed.

Rufus started to climb up the rigging, trying to see what the excitement was about. Celie pulled him back down and hopped onto his back, letting him carry her up around the crow's nest to watch. The boy doing the signaling called out the other ship's message to her, and she took it down to Orlath while the boy kept on passing news to the other ship.

"It's true," Celie said, landing next to Orlath at the wheel. "They've just come from Larien. They're warning us that we need to change course to avoid the Well."

"I wonder what they were doing in Larien," Lulath said in Grathian. "We don't do a great deal of trade with them."

"And more important: Did they see any unicorns?" Lilah put in. She was perched atop a barrel, sewing some of the blue fabric they'd bought in NeiMai.

"I don't know that there's a signal for unicorn," Orlath told her. He sighed and tugged at the wheel. "And I don't think we'll get close enough to talk more comfortably."

"What will we do?" Celie asked anxiously.

"Celie," Rolf said, "you do realize you're sitting on an animal that can *fly*, right?"

"Oh," Celie said. "Right."

"I am feeling the veriest fool," Lulath said. "Lorcan! Lorcan!" he shouted from the rail.

Lorcan was in the bow with Juliet, where they were allowing Jocko to run his tiny fingers through their feathers. The griffin looked up when his master called, though, and soon came flapping over to the rear deck. Juliet followed, and Celie came to the realization that Lorcan and Juliet, like their riders, were also in love.

So they decided on a delegation of Lulath, Lilah, Celie, and Queen Celina, who would ride double with Celie. Pogue would stay with Rolf and Orlath on the ship, which made Rolf grumble that he never got to go anywhere or do anything.

"My darling," Queen Celina said. "Do you realize how frantic with worry your father must be? Do you realize what a risk this is for Sleyne, to have all three heirs on one ship?"

"It is being true that there are being the pirates who fly the flag of my Grath," Lulath admitted. He was strapping on a sword.

"Then I should go, with a sword, and not Celie," Rolf protested.

"I'm sure they wouldn't attack women," Queen Celina said.

"You'd have to ride someone else's griffin," Pogue reminded him. "And, to be honest, Rolf, Celie speaks Grathian better than you."

Rolf huffed, but he had to admit that was true. He tried one last time, though.

"But I speak Grathian better than Lilah," he pointed out. "Lilah should stay, and I'll ride Juliet."

"Juliet hates that," Lilah said.

"Then I'll ride Arrow," Rolf retorted.

"I don't think Arrow would like that," Pogue said.

Rolf scowled, but he slumped down on the barrel that Lilah had vacated. They got on their griffins and took off for the other ship. Above them in the crow's nest, the boy was signaling that they were sending over a party.

This must have been highly confusing to the other ship, Celie thought as they swiftly crossed the ocean between them. They were probably expecting *The Golden Griffin* to turn and move toward them, and then a few people would row over in one of the smaller boats that hung alongside. But instead a trio of winged beasts was headed straight for their ship, and the *Griffin* wasn't changing course at all.

"Oh, my," Queen Celina said in Celie's ear as they flew over the water. She was holding tight around Celie's waist.

"Are you all right?" Celie asked her.

"Never better," her mother said. "Look at the fish!"

Looking down over Rufus's shoulder, Celie could see the silver fish just beneath the surface of the dark-blue water. They were darting about as though they were one body. She had to smile, too. And then they were there, with the pale-yellow sails of the other ship looming above them.

The deck of the Grathian ship, which was called the *Kraken*, was in turmoil when they arrived. The sailors were divided into two groups: those standing at the rail and gaping at the approaching griffins, and those running about the deck in a panic. The man whom Celie judged to be the captain was standing on the upper deck with his hands on his hips.

Celie decided he was the captain because of the amount of gold braid on his tunic. He was simply dripping with it. Also, lace. And his hair had been teased up into a silvery-gray cloud atop his head, which was very striking in contrast to his dark skin.

Lulath led them over to hover just over the rail beside

the upper deck so that he could address the man. Celie was right. He was the captain.

"Most noble captain of the mighty ship *Kraken*," Lulath called in Grathian. "We come to you from the noble ship *The Golden Griffin*, newly launched, and beg you to let us alight on your deck to speak with you."

"What are these creatures?" the captain thundered. "Are they the griffins of fable and legend?"

"Indeed, noble captain!"

"But we were told that only the royal families of Grath and Sleyne to the north had such beasts!" His eyes widened as realization dawned. "Please land, Your Noble Highnesses," he cried, bowing low.

They landed on the deck in a row in front of him. He bowed very low again. They all nodded politely, and Lulath introduced them, using very formal language that Celie could barely follow, and listing all their titles, much as he had with his parents when they'd arrived at the Sanctuary.

The captain bowed again and introduced himself as Captain Horvath-Atta, of the good ship *Kraken*, which was in fact returning from Larien. He frowned and then bowed again after saying this.

"I am sure that you, noble prince, and the good captain of your ship, are great sailors and know these waters well," he said uneasily. "But I must say that I, too, have sailed these seas for many years. And I must warn you, in good conscience, that you are steering straight for that dangerous whirlpool known as the Well." He said the name in a hushed tone, looking around as though making certain his men didn't hear him.

"Yes, we know," Lulath said airily. "We will turn when the time is right for us."

The crew were gathered at the edge of the upper deck, gaping. And now their master was standing there on the upper deck, mouth also hanging open.

"Do you not understand?" the captain whispered. "There is nothing more dangerous on this earth than the Well! You cannot even know if you are close to it, until you fall in!"

"We will not fall in," Lulath said. He spread his hands. "Truly, all will be well."

Celie hoped she looked as confident as Lulath. She hoped they all did, but didn't dare to check.

"I suppose, noble prince, that you know what is best for your ship," Captain Horvath-Atta said. But he didn't sound at all convinced.

"But we have a question for you," Lulath said, "which is why we flew across."

"Of course, my prince," the captain said. "Will you dismount and join me in a light refreshment?"

"We truly should not, though it is so generous of you to offer," Lulath said.

Celie looked over her shoulder. Their Ship had not stopped, and was rapidly moving away from the *Kraken*.

When she turned back she saw that Captain Horvath-Atta was also looking at *The Golden Griffin*, and seemed almost as stunned by it as he was by the griffins.

"What question do you have?" he asked, appearing truly nervous for the first time. "We have had some small success in Larien, but I do not know that we have anything that would be of any use to you."

"Oh, we shouldn't think to ask you to give us anything," Lulath said, appearing genuinely distressed.

"That was just right," Lilah said, urging Juliet a little to the front. "We really only very need to know one thing: Are there being unicorns in Land of Waterfalls?"

Captain Horvath-Atta blinked several times. Celie wasn't sure if it was Lilah's rather rocky Grathian or surprise at the question itself.

"Unicorns?"

"Yes," Celie said. "Creatures like horses, but with a horn." She put one finger to her forehead and mimed a horn jutting out.

The captain smiled at that. "I do know what unicorns are," he assured her. "But I simply didn't think to be asked such a question." He pursed his lips and thought. "I, of course, know of the unicorns, because it was a many-times great-grandfather of mine who was lost with the second ship."

"Second ship?" Lilah asked. "What is this meaning?"

"Are you sure you will not have refreshments?"

A tall man in a spotless white apron had come to the

upper deck. He was carrying a tray covered with tiny seed cakes, and behind him was a boy in a white apron with a pewter pitcher and a stack of cups.

"Oh, how nice," Queen Celina said.

She climbed off Rufus's back. As if it had been a pre-arranged signal, more of the crew swarmed the upper deck, bringing small stools, and they all dismounted and sat down. The ship's cook served them tiny cakes and cups of fruit juice, which were both delicious.

Except that Celie couldn't concentrate on them. She was too busy keeping one eye on the Ship, and the other on Horvath-Atta, who nibbled a cake and then took a large drink before settling in to tell the story.

"You know, I suppose, that the ships left Grath many centuries ago, to take the unicorns from our lands to a place of safety?"

"Ships?" Lilah asked. "We have been hearing of the only *one* ship."

The captain was already shaking his head. He held up two long, brown fingers, decorated with gold rings. "*Two*, fair princess. Unicorns are large; they could not take them all on one vessel, though many of the beasts had been lost along the way. They were not tame, but wild animals, hunted and chased—getting them onto the ships was not easy, from what I have been told.

"Two ships set out for Larien, but only one reached it." Captain Horvath-Atta looked past them at *The Golden Griffin* and grimaced. "The other ship, the one captained by my ancestor, veered too close to the Well and was drawn in."

They all froze, and then Lilah tossed her hair back. "So it has truth? That there have been unicorns at Larien?" she asked.

"One ship reached Larien. But the unicorns did not thrive there," Captain Horvath-Atta told them. "I saw one on my first journey there. I was only a boy. It was beautiful, but so fragile. They have all died now."

"All?" Lilah asked in a small voice.

"I am afraid so, Your Highness," the captain said.

"So ridiculous that they didn't bring them back to Sleyne, once the griffins were gone," Queen Celina said.

"The griffins, Your Majesty?" He gave the creatures a puzzled look.

"The griffins in Sleyne all died out as well," Queen Celina said. "Not long after the ships sailed. I don't understand why someone didn't bring the unicorns back then."

"There were griffins in Sleyne then?" Captain Horvath-Atta looked completely mystified. "Are you certain, Your Majesty? I have never heard such a thing!"

"Then why did they load them onto ships and take them to Larien?" Celie asked. "If they weren't being hunted by the griffins?"

"Hunted? No," he said, shaking his head. "The one I saw was too delicate to do any harm, but in the old days they were powerful hunters, and very dangerous. They were herded to the docks and sent away because people feared them so much."

Now it was their turn to blink at him, confused.

"Oh," Celie said.

"Yes," the captain said, nodding. "The Magistrate of Larien said he would take them, because many of the isles have no people on them, and there the monsters could do no harm." He shook his head sadly. "They had killed so many of your people, you see."

"Oh," Celie said again.

"Thank you so for these many cakes," Lilah said, rising. "We are to be going."

Chapter
19

⟨≈⟩

It took two weeks to reach the Well.

Celie didn't know why everyone had panicked and told them to steer east or west when the Ship first aimed its course toward the Well. Two weeks was more than enough time to go either way. But they'd passed three more ships whose crews had thought themselves very daring indeed for going so close to the whirlpool, and all of whom had warned *The Golden Griffin* crew to alter their course. They had brushed these warnings aside, while secretly their terror had mounted. There seemed to be no room for doubt: the Ship was headed for the Well.

"Which we've taken two weeks to catch sight of," Celie grumbled to Rolf. "Two weeks moving at our fastest speed. It would have taken any other ship three weeks at least, but everyone warned us away. Why is everyone so afraid of this Well?"

Rolf shrugged. There was still nothing to see. They only knew they were near the Well because of the direction of the tides and the position of the stars overhead. As far as any of the Glowers could tell, they were surrounded by nothing more sinister than water, though the crew all looked at that water with great suspicion.

"I'm sure it will all be nothing," Rolf said. "Maybe it's just a myth that the Well even exists. We'll probably just sail right through completely calm waters and come out on the other side."

They were both slumped on barrels, leaning on the bow rail. Rufus and Dagger were diving into the water alongside the bow, trying to snatch up fish. When they did find them, they would throw them onto the deck, and Rolf would smack the fish on the head and throw them into a basket. Lorcan, Arrow, and Juliet had a net they liked to drag through the water to catch larger fish, but Rufus and Dagger preferred to do it with their bare talons.

"I just think someone told a wild story about there being an enormous whirlpool here," Celie said idly. One of her arms was dangling over the rail so she could snap her fingers at Rufus if he dove too close to the prow of the ship. They were going so fast that the sailors had warned Celie about how easy it would be for the griffins to get caught in the wake and dragged under. "You know, the way sailors do, and then everyone took them seriously and started marking it on maps, and—"

Celie sat bolt upright.

"*Rufus! Get out of the water!*" she screamed.

Rolf lurched to his feet. He looked over the side and let out a yell that turned into his own griffin's name. "Dagger! *Dagger!*"

"What is it?" Pogue was at the bow immediately.

Celie's eyes were still on Rufus, who was circling nearby in confusion. Celie pointed to the water, silently urging Pogue to look, as she gave Rufus a sharp command to come. She didn't take her eyes off her griffin until he'd landed beside her, and then she turned to see if Pogue had seen it, too.

It was clear from his white face that Pogue had seen the sudden change in the water, and it had terrified him as well. When Dagger teased Rolf by flying past him, just above the rail, and then back out over the sea, Pogue gave his own sharp whistle and command. When Dagger flew close again, Rolf snatched a handful of his tail, and Pogue managed to grab the young griffin's harness and bring him down to the deck.

"What's going on up here?" Lilah said, coming forward to see what they were all shouting about. "Did you see one of those fish with a sword nose?"

They didn't even have to answer her. As soon as the word "nose" left her mouth she fell silent. Her hands clutched at the rail.

"The water is black," Lilah whispered.

"Yes," Celie said, her stomach churning. "And green."

But not a normal, healthy green. No, the water was slick and black and strange-looking, and the crests of the waves, where the foam was usually white, were a poisonous shade of green. It reminded Celie of the deadly lake in Hatheland, and she could see that Rolf and Lilah were having the same reaction.

The crew, too, though none of them had ever been to Hatheland, were panicking. They ran about the deck without their usual purpose, and several of them climbed the rigging with frantic movements—trying to get farther from the water, Celie suspected.

Queen Celina came rushing toward them now. She was blinking owlishly at the water, and her hair was pinned up with a couple of pencils. She had been in her cabin, studying Orlath's maps, and she had to shield her eyes from the sudden brightness of the sun.

"It's black," the queen said. "When did this happen?"

"We are in the pull of the Well," Orlath told them when he arrived at the bow with Lulath at his heels. "The boy in the crow's nest spotted the change in color earlier." He was pale, and his voice was low with studied calm.

"And we still cannot turn?" Queen Celina asked.

"We've been trying all morning," Pogue said grimly. "Harder than before. And we've added magic, and prayers, to our physical strength."

"Magic?" Queen Celina's voice was sharp. "What magic? I certainly haven't done anything!"

"Just the usual spells and charms that sailors carry," Orlath assured her. "And Lilah and Lulath and Pogue have spent the morning entreating the Ship." He rubbed a hand over his face, and Celie wondered when he'd last slept. "But the Ship will not turn. And now it cannot turn."

"Not just this morning," Lilah said shrilly. "We've spent *days* begging the Ship to change course!"

"Lilah," her mother said, stroking back her daughter's dark curls from her flushed face, "we've been over this time and again: the Ship must know what it's doing."

"I don't think it does," Lilah said, pulling away from her mother. "I think it's trying to kill us all!"

"No, my Lilah!" Lulath protested. "Surely that is not being its purpose!"

"But what if it is?"

"We're moving," Rolf shouted.

"Yes, Rolf, we *know*," Lilah snapped.

"I mean we're moving *sideways*," Rolf snapped back.

Rolf was right: the Ship was moving sideways, slowly. They were caught in the Well, and now there truly was no turning back. Even if the Ship had wanted to, Celie didn't think it could change course now.

There was a great creaking and groaning, and the sails began to whip around.

"She's trying to turn," Orlath said in a hushed voice. "She's trying to keep her course straight."

"What do we do?" Pogue said. "How can we help?"

"Come to the helm with me," Orlath said, and started to turn away.

A loose rope whipped across the bow, and Rufus leaped up and snatched hold of it, yanking on it as if it were a tug-o-war rope from his tower at the Castle.

Orlath's face brightened. More of the ropes were whipping loose as the Ship tried to adjust its sails, and the sailors, confused and frightened, were all hunched at the base of the mast.

"What do I do?" Celie said at once.

"Mount up," Orlath said, as though she were a knight and Rufus her steed.

Which, she supposed, was true. She leaped onto his back and settled herself, telling him to keep hold of the rope but not bite through it as she did so.

"Tie that to the spar there," he ordered, pointing, "so that the sail is pulled on an angle, that way." He pointed in the opposite direction. "All of you: mount up! Let's get these sails secured." He saw Pogue and hesitated. "No, on your griffin," he said. "Rolf, to the helm!"

Rufus seemed to know just what to do, and Celie barely had to guide him as he flew up to hover near the spar Orlath had pointed to. Celie leaned over Rufus's neck and grabbed the trailing end of the rope. Then she hauled it in with both hands, pulling the striped sail taut with great effort. She wrapped the rope around the spar and tied it the way one of the crew had shown her during some of the more boring days on the Ship.

Across the way she could see Lilah and Juliet doing the same thing to another sail rope, and below were Lulath and Lorcan with two ropes that held the largest sail. Lorcan had one rope in his mouth, while Lulath had another in his hand, and they were flying straight out from the Ship, trying to drag the canvas as far to the west as they could before tying it off.

Once they had all the sails tied into place, the Ship was still groaning and straining, but they were moving forward more than to the side. Orlath and Rolf both had their hands on the wheel. They were turning it—or, rather, keeping it turned—so that the rudder was at an angle, too.

Celie didn't know what else to do, so she guided Rufus to go up higher, away from the Ship, so that they could see the Well. Once they had a good view of it, Rufus froze in the air, forgetting to flap his wings. It wasn't until they started to fall rather than glide that Celie came to her senses and shouted for him to keep them in the air.

The Well was enormous. And horrible. A great sucking hole in the sea, with nothing but black water swirling around the edge and black nothingness in the center.

Celie knew she was one of a handful of people to have seen the Well from above. And the only others were with her: Pogue, Lilah, and Lulath. They were all flying high, ahead of the bow of the Ship, and looking down into the Well. It wasn't even water down at the bottom, from what Celie could tell. It was just . . . nothing.

She shuddered, and when she gave the command for Rufus to land on the Ship, he dove for the main deck so swiftly that she slipped back a little and had to grip him tighter with her legs to keep from falling.

Rufus landed with a thump right at the foot of the mast, and Celie staggered off his back. Her mother was there, doing something magical to the base of the mast, and spared only a glance at Celie to make certain she was all right. The others landed around her, and they all stood beside their griffins in silence and watched as Queen Celina finished painting wizardly markings around the mast.

"How bad is it?" she asked when she was done.

"It's . . . bad," Celie said.

"We're going to die," Lilah agreed, but in a subdued way. Lulath put an arm around her, drawing her close to his side. "We should . . . we should have Orlath marry us. Right now. He can do that, can't he?" she asked Lulath.

"I shouldn't think we need to do something so dramatic," Queen Celina said. "And besides, you all need to leave immediately."

"What do you mean, Your Majesty?" Pogue was the one to ask.

"I don't know why we didn't think of it before," the queen said, almost cheerfully. "Especially when those other ships were closer! But you can all ride your griffins away from here."

"What are you saying?" Lilah demanded.

"I'm saying that we're going to put as many as we can on the griffins, and ride them away from here," Queen Celina said patiently.

"But we can only carry a couple of people," Celie spluttered. "Rolf, you, Orlath . . . What about the crew?"

"I've reinforced the Ship as best I can," the queen said. "To give us a better chance."

"Us?" Celie asked with deep suspicion.

"Well, someone has to stay with the Ship," she said. "Orlath is insisting that as the captain, it should be him."

Lulath made a sound of distress.

"But since I'm the only one who can use magic, I thought it had better be me," she finished, still smiling.

"No," Celie said, barely able to whisper the word.

"I'm going to speak to my brother," Lulath said in Grathian, looking dazed.

"Celie," her mother said as Lilah and Lulath hurried aft to the Ship's wheel to speak to Orlath. "You have to go. You and Rolf. You know this." Now there was a hint of pleading in her voice.

"I agree," Pogue said gruffly. He tried to lift Celie onto Rufus's back, but she dodged away.

"Stop that," she snapped. He'd done it before, and it had saved her life. But this was not the time for her to be flying off free, while her family and the entire crew *died*. "I'm not going unless we all go."

"At the very least, Your Majesty," Pogue said, "I think

we could impose on Lady Griffin to carry you and someone else. That will allow two more people to escape."

"Did you really just say that?" Celie demanded. "There are almost two dozen men on the Ship! I'm not leaving them to die!"

Several of the crew jerked around and stared at the sound of Celie's voice, and one of them swore. The first mate started toward them, pushed forward by his fellows, but Queen Celina held up one hand and shook her head, smiling all the while.

"Celie," she whispered. "Don't fight me on this. You need to get out of here. You and Rolf and Lilah. And Pogue and Lulath. I don't even care about Orlath . . . but you children need to go." Her smile never faltered, but her voice broke at the end. "Go, darling! Before it's too late."

Celie started crying. Her mother gave a signal to Pogue, and he dumped her across Rufus's back like a sack of potatoes. She tried to fight him but couldn't, so instead she slithered off as soon as he let go.

"I don't want to go," Celie pleaded. "I—"

She fell sideways across Rufus's back again. Pogue had taken the opportunity to boost her back up. Then he almost knocked her right back off when he fell against Rufus.

The Ship was deep into the Well now. Even with the sails and the wheel turned to make their course as straight as possible, they were swirling around with the pull of the water. The force of it made everything and everyone tilt sideways. The crew were lurching about, shouting and cursing. Arrow spread his legs and dug into the deck with his talons, but Rufus pressed himself against the mast, which was the only way that Celie could get herself upright on his back and take hold of the harness.

Queen Celina was pressed against the mast now, too. She crouched and then sat, her back against the tall wooden column. Her face looked strained, and Celie knew that her mother was using magic somehow, even as she shooed Celie and Rufus away.

"Go now, darling," she said with her jaw clenched. "Just go."

"I can't leave you!" Celie said. Then another thought struck her. "The puppies!"

Down below in Rolf's cabin were Lulath's girls and the puppies. Celie had hardly seen them since they'd been born. Kitsi kept them close, and the other dogs stood watch and made sure the new mother had her pick of their food.

"I'll get the puppies," Pogue said. "Just go!"

But Celie couldn't. And neither could Pogue. None of them could move now.

The force of the whirlpool was pressing them against the deck. Celie had to slide down off Rufus's back and let the momentum paste her to the mast beside her mother. Rufus stretched out his legs until he was pinned to the deck with his limbs and wings painfully outspread.

The Ship was tilted now, the bow pointing down, and loose ropes and barrels were falling into the Well.

Celie could see it rising up around them as the Ship angled toward the blackness at the center and began to race down.

Down.

Down.

Into the nothingness.

Chapter
20

~⚬~

Everything was blackness. There was a feeling of being pressed, hard, against the deck of the Ship, which was what saved them. Celie couldn't see anything, but she could feel that the Ship was now standing up on its prow, with the griffin figurehead going straight down into the heart of the Well. All she could do was grip her mother with one hand and Rufus's harness with the other and pray.

There was an intense pressure building in her ears, and a terrible sound as though the ship were breaking apart. Then with a pop like a wine cork her ears cleared, and the Ship righted itself.

Celie felt light on her eyelids, and opened her eyes. She hadn't remembered closing them. But once she opened them, she closed them again. Then she tried opening them once more, but that didn't change anything.

They were in another world. There was no doubt about it. It was nighttime here, whereas it had been noon when they'd struck the Well. And it wasn't just that the time of day had changed: there were two moons hanging low in the sky, and one of them was distinctly pink in color. And although Celie had never been interested in astronomy, even she could see that the stars formed new constellations.

Queen Celina sat up straight and then stood, using Rufus to pull herself up with a groan. Then she, too, noticed the strange sky and gasped.

"Is this Hatheland?" she asked, gazing around in fascination.

"No," Celie said, sliding her back up the mast until she was on her feet. "It's not." She looked around. Pogue was sprawled across Arrow's back, and she hurried around the still-shaky Rufus to help him up. "Are you all right?"

"I managed not to get knocked out this time," Pogue said with a smile, straightening. He looked around. "This isn't home," he said. He looked at the pink moon. "And it isn't Hatheland, either."

"How exciting!" Queen Celina said. "But where are the others?" She raised her voice. "Rolf? Lilah? Lulath?"

"Here!" Lilah called, waving her arm.

She was standing near the wheel. So were Rolf, Lulath, and Orlath. Grouped around them, shaking out their feathers and making irritated noises, were Lorcan and Juliet, but there was no sign of Dagger or Lady Griffin. Queen Celina noticed this at once.

"Lady? My lady?" she called. She clapped her hands. "Lady!"

"Dagger's below," Rolf called. "I'll look for her, too." He leaped off the aft deck and down into the hold.

"Where are we?" Lilah said. She, too, was gazing at the pink moon.

The first mate came over to Celie and her mother. "Yes, um, Highnesses?" he asked, uneasy. "We were wondering that. Where . . . where are we?"

"We don't know," Queen Celina told him.

The first mate stared at her. He was clearly near to panicking, and could not understand why she was smiling so widely. They were lost, and in a strange world. Several of the crew were still sitting on the deck, and Celie heard one man openly sobbing.

"We will speak with Prince Orlath," Celie announced loudly. "But the good news is that the Ship is still whole and no one was injured." She looked around quickly. "No one was injured? Were they?"

The man brightened. "I will check on every crewman," he told her. "If it pleases Your Majesty?" He gave the queen an uncertain look.

"A wonderful idea," Queen Celina told him warmly. "And why don't you gather everyone here on the main deck, and in a few minutes we will make an announcement."

The man nodded and hurried away.

"I'm going to go to the bow and look around," Celie said.

"I'll go with her," Pogue said.

"And I'm going to consult with Orlath," Queen Celina said. She threw her arms around Celie and gave her a quick hug. "I can't believe I'm in another world," she said. "I've been so jealous of you children! And now I get to come on an adventure as well!"

Celie didn't know what to say, so she just nodded and guided Rufus to the bow. She heard Pogue grab Arrow, who was still clinging to the deck with his talons, and drag him along behind.

"How . . . I just . . . ," Celie stammered when she reached the bow and Pogue had joined her.

"I can see her point," Pogue said cautiously. "You and Rolf and Lilah, and, well, I, have been on a lot of adventures. We've been to two strange worlds now—"

"She went to Hatheland with us, to find the griffin eggs," Celie pointed out.

"For a day," Pogue countered. "And that was after the adventure part was finished and everything was ash."

"All right, that's true," Celie admitted. "But soon the excitement will wear off, and she'll find out that adventures are nothing but being cold and tired and hungry and scared all the time."

Pogue laughed, but more like he agreed with her. Together they stood in the bow and surveyed the world around them in silence. The two moons and the stars, which seemed closer than the stars at home, made things bright enough to see that they were on another ocean. The water still looked blackish, but the foam had a pink tint thanks to the smaller moon. And off to starboard there was—

"Is that . . . ?" Celie said, and then stopped to lean farther over the bow rail.

"Land," Pogue said. "It's land."

"It is," Celie said. "It is!"

"Land!" Pogue shouted, pointing.

It was a thin white line of beach running along the horizon. Beyond it the darkness was more green than black, and too irregular to be waves.

Behind Celie the crew were scrambling around, and so was her family. She didn't see any point in getting in the way, however, so she stayed in the bow and kept her eyes on the land, just in case it was only a vision.

"The Ship isn't moving under its own power anymore," Lilah said when she joined Celie in the bow. "Orlath will have to actually sail us into the port."

"Is there a port?" Celie asked, but she knew the answer. Scanning the dimly lit shore, she could see only sand and what she decided must be a thick forest.

"You know what I mean," Lilah said.

The lamps on the Ship were lit, and the men were moving about with purpose now. Several of them scrambled up into the rigging to bring the sails about, and at the helm Orlath was shouting orders. The wind caught the sails, and the captain was able to turn the wheel at last, bringing the Ship around and aiming it straight at the dimly seen shore.

"This is where those ships have been going," Celie said as they drew closer to the shore. "Don't you think? All those ships that disappeared over the years, falling into the Well . . . they came *here*."

Lilah gripped Celie's arm, her face absolutely glowing in the lamplight.

"That would be truly an amazing thing," Lulath said gently. "But there is the small problem that so many ships have been lost here."

"And?" Celie said, not seeing the problem.

"And yet there is nothing here. No dock. No other ships in sight. Not even any wreckage," Lulath said. His voice was still gentle, and low so that it didn't carry to the crew.

"What do you think happened to them, then?" Celie asked.

"I'm thinking that they didn't make it through the Well," Lulath said. "It may be that we made it because of our wonderful Ship, and your mother's magic."

"That can't be possible," Lilah said. "I refuse to accept that!" She shook her head vehemently.

"Why?" Rolf said, coming up to them. His tunic was writhing, and it took Celie a moment to realize that he had the puppies inside it. "What are you not accepting?"

"I'm not accepting that we're the only ship to have made it through the Well to this world," Lilah restated. "Because if we are, then that means . . ." She let her voice trail away.

"That means the unicorns really are all dead," Celie finished for her.

"Yes," Lilah whispered. "And we're stuck in this world for nothing."

"Still," Rolf said, "it's a new world. There might be anything here, like more griffins, or a different kind of unicorn. Or dragons!"

"I don't want to be anywhere near a dragon," Lilah said. "They breathe fire and eat people!"

"Well, apparently unicorns aren't that nice, either," Rolf reminded her. "All this time we've been worried that the griffins would eat them, and that our ancestors were the reason they left Sleyne. It turns out that they were just horrible to begin with!"

"It doesn't matter; they're all dead anyway," Lilah moaned.

"All right, children," Queen Celina said, coming to the bow. "It's time to stop bickering."

"And do what?" Celie asked. "Are we really going to try to reach the shore in the dark?"

Along with there being no sign of any people (or unicorns) on the shore, there was also no sign of a lighthouse or any markers showing where rocks might be. It would be too awful if the Ship made it through the Well and into another world, only to sink on a rock within sight of land.

That seemed to be Orlath's fear as well. Now that they were turned in the right direction, the crew were furling the sails and dropping anchor. Queen Celina had come to tell her family that it was time for them all to get to bed.

"A nice rest, and in the morning we'll explore this new world," she told them brightly, as though sleep was easy to accomplish in such circumstances.

"But what about Lady Griffin?" Rolf asked, transferring some of the puppies to Lulath's tunic and giving another to Celie to cuddle.

"What about her?" Queen Celina looked around with her brow furrowed. "Wait—where is she, Rolf? I thought you found her!"

"That's just it," Rolf said. "I got distracted by the puppies when I came back on deck, but there was no sign of her below."

"Has anyone seen her since we came through the Well?" Queen Celina asked.

They all shook their heads.

It seemed that Lady Griffin was gone.

Chapter 21

Celie woke up the next morning feeling more exhausted than when she'd lain down. Her eyes were sticky and swollen, her mouth was dry, and she had a pounding headache. One look at Lilah told her that her sister hadn't fared much better. Celie had cried herself to sleep, and she was sure Lilah had done the same.

Queen Celina had performed a searching spell, but there was no sign of Lady Griffin. She was just gone, and none of them could remember whether they'd seen her come through the Well or not. If she'd fallen off the Ship in this world, she would have flown right back on, so it was likely that she hadn't come through at all. Which meant that, if she wasn't drowned, she was alone at the edge of the Well.

A fresh wave of sobs came over Celie, and she hurried to try to scrub her face and eyes at the washbasin. Lilah was standing there with a wet cloth in one hand, her hair matted around her face and her eyes nearly swollen shut.

"Even if she didn't drown, no one will come near enough to rescue her," Lilah said. "How far can she fly? She won't be able to reach land. Could she fly far enough to reach one of the ships we passed?" Her voice was dull, and Celie knew that she wasn't really asking, just repeating the same thing over and over that Celie had heard in her own mind all night.

"She's the queen of the griffins," Celie said, with as much conviction as she could muster. "She'll be fine."

She tried to make her words more convincing by going about her morning ablutions: combing her hair and washing her face, which did make her feel better. She put on one of the simple gowns that she and Lilah had made from the blue cloth they'd bought in NeiMai. Lilah shook herself and fixed Celie's hair and her own, though she looked very unlike herself in her plain gown and with her thick hair braided away from her face.

No one had much appetite for breakfast, but the sight of the shore made them feel a little more cheerful. Or at least it took their attention away from their loss.

With the sun up, they had weighed anchor and unfurled the sails, under the command of an equally tired-looking Orlath. The shore was fast approaching, revealing a white-sand beach skirting a green landscape. There were men posted in the bow and the crow's nest, looking for rocks, but the water was surprisingly clear. They could see schools of exotic fish and forests of underwater plants despite the blackish tinge to the water.

But soon they had to drop anchor again. There was a shelf of sand extending out from the shore, and the water was not deep enough for them to continue. Celie stayed in the bow while the crew settled the anchor and the sails, gazing into the thick trees that obscured the land ahead.

Then she saw it. A flash of silvery white in the green trees.

"Rufus," Celie called without taking her eyes off the spot.

Everyone else was fussing about, discussing how many of the small boats they should take and who would go and who would stay on the Ship. Rolf was pointing out that the griffins should fly over and leave more room for people in the boats when he saw Celie swinging her leg over Rufus's back, her gaze still locked on the shore.

"I'm with Celie," Rolf said. "We should head over there on the griffins first, to make sure it's even safe to step on the land." He quickly hopped onto Rufus behind Celie before she could say anything.

"Just hang on," she muttered, and gave Rufus the signal to fly.

"Land over there," Rolf said, pointing over her shoulder.

"No," Celie told him. "I know where I'm going."

She'd seen it again: the white flicker between the trees. There was a large moss-covered rock, then a tree that was bent over it, as though it were trying to grow around the rock. The flicker had been just to the left of them, both times.

"There's more flat sand to land on if we go to the right," Rolf said.

"I saw something," Celie told him. "Over there." She pointed, and he clasped her tighter around the waist in excitement. Something squirmed against her back. "What is that?" She tried to twist around, and Rufus squawked in disapproval.

"Sapuppy," Rolf said.

"What?"

"It's a puppy," he said more clearly.

"What?"

"It's a puppy," he said again.

"Why do you have a puppy in your shirt?" Celie twisted around as much as she could and caught a glimpse of a small white-and-brown head peeking out from the collar of Rolf's blue shirt.

He shrugged. "Lulath asked me to. We were looking for you to take one as well," he said.

They were almost to the shore. The water was a pleasant pale green here, and the sand could clearly be seen under its surface, strewn with oddly shaped shells. Rufus soared down and landed neatly just beyond the water, on the stretch of sand right in front of the mossy rock.

Up close the sand wasn't all that white, but freckled with black and red specks, as though it were salt mixed with a little pepper and another spice. The farther from the water they went, the more dark specks there were, until it blended into the black soil and rocks.

"With Lady Griffin . . . being gone, it made him nervous that we might lose the puppies as well," Rolf explained. "So Lulath wants everyone to keep the dogs close." He slipped off Rufus's back and adjusted his belt so that the puppy could see out without scrambling around. "Now, the important thing is: What did you see?"

"I don't know," Celie said. "But it was white, and it was right here." She pointed to the crooked tree.

She started to get off Rufus, but Rolf waved for her to stay on. He drew his sword, which looked highly incongruous with the puppy peeking out of his clothes. He stepped in front of Celie and Rufus, which was irritating, but since the others were on their way to the shore, she decided not to waste time complaining. Using his sword to sweep vines and branches aside, Rolf led the way into the dense forest.

The trees were strange. The vines were strange. Even the rocks were of a type that Celie had never seen before: porous, jagged-edged, and black beneath the moss that grew on them. The moss also grew on the ground and the trees, and she worried that if Rufus stopped moving, it would grow on him, too.

They hacked their way past the crooked tree and into the forest, and a green silence closed over them. They could no longer hear the ocean, or the cries of Lilah and

Pogue, calling for them to wait. All Celie heard was the soft squish of the moss under Rufus's feet, the slice of Rolf's sword through the vines, and the occasional squeak from the puppy.

Rolf was trying to be as quiet as possible, which Celie appreciated. She didn't know what she'd seen: animal, bird, or human, and any one of those things might be wary of humans. They would certainly be wary of griffins. She just hoped they didn't hide so completely that they never found another living soul on this island.

"Wait," Celie whispered as something occurred to her. "Is this an island? Or a continent?"

Rolf stopped. "I don't know," he whispered. "I mean, how big does it have to be before you say that it's a continent?"

"Big," said a voice from the tree above them.

Celie screamed, and Rufus leaped back, his wings rising up and his front right talon poised to strike. Rolf whipped around so fast that he tripped on a vine and fell on his rump. The puppy took the opportunity to wiggle free, but all it could do was roll off Rolf's lap and then sit on the moss and cry.

Celie craned her neck back, but there was nothing to be seen in the branches above her head. She stuck her feet into the straps of Rufus's harness and tried to stand up so that she could get a better look, but Rufus lurched forward.

He stepped right over Rolf before he could get up, and Celie dragged on the harness, but he wouldn't stop. She was about to give him an order, loudly, when she heard something. It was coming from the tree in front of and above them.

"Bigger than a ship, smaller than a world," said the voice in the tree. Then the tree rustled, and Rufus charged ahead.

"Get up," Celie called over her shoulder to Rolf.

"I'm trying," he shouted as she left him behind.

Rufus followed the rustling of leaves and the occasional laugh from whoever it was taunting them. And Celie knew they were being taunted. There was no doubt about it. Whoever it was didn't have to laugh in that pointed way. They didn't have to rustle the leaves so loudly. They were leaping from tree to tree in complete silence and without revealing themselves at all, so the laugh and rustle were purely to tell Celie where they were.

"Celie, stop! It's a trap," Rolf called.

"I know, but we need to talk to them," Celie cried. "Please stop! Please help us!"

"Why?" the voice asked, curious.

"Because our Ship is—"

Rufus stumbled over one last root and through some trees, and Celie stopped short. They were in a little clearing, the ground sunken like a bowl and lined only with moss. There was no sign of whomever they had been following.

"Please help us," Celie said again, craning her neck to try to see any movement from the trees. "Our Ship came here from another world! We fell through the Well, and we . . ." She closed her eyes, still tired and itchy after her restless night. "We need to get back. Please."

Wheezing, Rolf caught up to her. He put his hands on his knees and tried to catch his breath.

"Are you all right?" the voice asked.

"Be all right in a minute," he gasped. "You speak Sleynth very well," he managed.

"We have your kind here," the voice said, clearly offended—and clearly a female, Celie could tell, now that she wasn't chasing her through the jungle.

"Our kind?" Celie asked.

"The Sleynth, by your talk. Also the Grathians, with their lace. The Neirans, all in blue. Like you. All people come here."

"But where are we?" Celie demanded. "And who are *you?*"

"Here is the Land," the voice said, impatient. "And I am one of the Found."

"Okay," Rolf said, finally straightening. He adjusted the puppy in his shirt. "So you're one of the found and you live in this land?"

"That's right."

"Then can you come down out of the trees so that we can introduce ourselves properly? We would like to see whom we're speaking to."

"I was about to," the voice said petulantly. "But you have attracted attention, and I'm not coming down until it's gone."

"What's gone?" Celie said, her scalp prickling.

"That."

Celie still didn't see anything, but Rufus could either see or smell something, and he didn't like it. He shifted beneath her, clacking his beak and clawing at the soft moss with his talons.

"Take this, would you?"

Rolf pulled the puppy out of his tunic and gave it to Celie. She stuck it down the front of her gown, which was a much tighter fit than Rolf's tunic, and held the puppy more securely. Rolf drew his sword again and moved close to Rufus.

Across the bowl of the clearing, a creature stepped into the light. It was white, and Celie wondered if it was what she had seen by the crooked tree. It was the size of a large deer, though more delicately boned. It gleamed, sleek and vividly pale, with huge dark eyes. The ivory horn that spiraled up from its forehead was easily as long as Celie's arm.

"Oh," Celie murmured as she stared at the unicorn. "Where is Lilah?"

"She's going to kill us when she finds out we saw one first," Rolf agreed.

He hadn't bothered to lower his voice, and the unicorn's head came up. It froze, and Celie and Rolf froze, while Celie silently cursed. Now it would run off, and they'd probably never see it again, and Lilah would be so disappointed!

But instead of fleeing, it lowered its head so that the horn was pointed right at them. And then it charged.

Rufus flew straight up in the air, screaming in terror. Not sure what else to do, Celie kicked at Rolf as she went past, hitting him squarely in the chest with her foot and knocking him flat.

The unicorn passed right under Rufus, narrowly missing Rolf with its hooves. It turned when it realized it hadn't struck either of them and prepared to charge again. Rufus wanted to go higher to avoid it, but Celie urged him down so that he could pick up Rolf with his talons. They wouldn't get far that way, but they could get away from this dreadful beast.

Rufus refused to go lower, however, and the unicorn charged before she could convince him. Celie screamed and Rolf rolled to one side, and then a brightly colored shape hurtled out of the trees and swung across the unicorn's path. The unicorn trumpeted in distress as a gold whip lashed its side. It spun on a single hoof and tore away into the forest.

The brightly colored shape shook itself and then helped Rolf to his feet. Rufus landed a few paces away, allowing Celie to get a look at their rescuer. She was a young woman of about Lilah's age, with very large blue eyes and very brown skin. She was covered from head to foot in layers of clothing that appeared to be woven out of ribbons in a rainbow of colors. Even her hair was covered with a headdress of dangling ribbons.

She coiled her golden whip and bowed.

"Now that you are out of danger, will you stay to meet the Master of the Found?" she asked.

"Um, I suppose we'd better," Celie replied.

Chapter
22

Queen Celina, Lilah, Lulath, and Pogue caught up to them as they left the clearing. They all had their griffins, save for Lady Griffin, and Lorcan had a basket of dogs hanging on either side of his harness. Celie gave the puppy in her gown back to its mother, but Jou-Jou would not be appeased, so Celie ended up carrying the larger dog in her arms as she sat on Rufus's back. The native girl watched this exchange without comment, and brushed aside their attempts at introductions as well.

"The Master of the Found will hear your names," was all she said, cutting off Queen Celina mid-introduction.

Whereas she'd been positively chatty when she was leading Celie and Rolf through the jungle, she was completely silent now, moving ahead of them through the green without stepping on a single dry twig or disturbing a hanging vine. Meanwhile the others came behind her, hacking at the vines and exclaiming over the strange foliage, the dogs barking at birds and the griffins carking their displeasure at the entire enterprise.

They were deep in the jungle now. Celie would have been nervous about being so far from the shore and the Ship, except that she had Rufus. They could fly away the moment things looked dangerous. It was greatly comforting.

There was a break in the trees ahead, and the girl stopped. When they caught up to her, they stopped talking. The griffins stopped squawking and fussing, and even the dogs were silent. For a moment, everything just . . . stopped.

Celie had thought that the clearing where they'd met the unicorn had been like a bowl, but it was nothing compared to this. The ground in front of them dropped away, and there was a wide, deep valley curving out as far as they could see. It was just as round and even as the clearing, but the ground below was covered with trees rather than just moss.

But that wasn't the most amazing part. No, the most amazing part was the city that had been built over the trees.

Rope bridges ran like a giant spiderweb across the valley, not even skimming the tops of the trees. The bridges connected large wooden platforms that had apparently been built on the very tops of the trees, and on the platforms were tents and wooden buildings of every shape and size and color, with woven ribbons fluttering from the peak of every roof and wound around the ropes of every bridge.

"So lovely," Queen Celina said. "So bright!"

"Thank you," the girl said with no small amount of pride. "The Found are fond of color."

"And of ships," Pogue said. He pointed to the nearest platform, which held a house that appeared to have been roofed with an upside-down rowboat and walled with sail canvas.

"Ironwoods are difficult to work with," the girl said, rubbing her hand over the smooth, silver trunk of the nearest tree. "So we use found."

"Your pardon?" Queen Celina said.

But the girl had surged ahead. She walked along the edge of the valley to the nearest rope bridge. There was a gate across it made of a net of ribbons, and she untied it with deft fingers and then stood aside, waiting for them.

Rufus walked to the head of the bridge, but then he carked his displeasure and backed away. The other griffins all took their cue from Rufus, and none of them would come any closer to the bridge, no matter how the humans prodded them.

"I can't really blame them," Rolf said, peering over the edge. "I mean, that's a long drop through some very aggressive trees."

"Where are we going?" Lilah demanded. "Rather than drag the griffins across these bridges, we're just going to have to fly to wherever it is."

"Suit yourself," the girl said. She pointed to a platform that held a very large, very orange tent. There were three bridges between them. "That is the Master of the Found's own place," she said.

"We'll just see you there, then," Rolf said. "Right, Rufus?"

Rufus moved around so that Rolf could mount behind Celie. Rolf hopped on, and Queen Celina got on Juliet behind Lilah. Lulath and Pogue had been walking alongside their griffins to give them a respite, but now they also mounted.

"Would you like to ride?" Pogue asked their guide politely.

"No," the girl said after considering for a moment. "Not right now."

She passed through the gate and then began to knot it closed again. Rufus decided that he was done waiting, and he leaped off the edge of the valley. Celie had to grip with her legs, because her arms were full of JouJou. Rolf grabbed hold around her waist, which also helped. Rufus soared down to skim the fluffy green treetops and then sailed back up again and landed neatly on the wooden platform beside the orange tent.

In an instant, guards had surrounded them. They were male and female, dressed in clothes woven of many-colored ribbon—which would have looked quite festive, if it weren't for the spears they were holding.

"We mean you no harm!" Rolf shouted, holding up his hands.

"How do you do?" Queen Celina said calmly, slipping off Juliet's back. She, too, held her hands out where they could see them, but in a very elegant way, as though she were about to fluff her skirts. "I am Queen Celina of Sleyne, and I'm here to meet with your Master of the Found."

"*She* brought us," Lilah blurted out, pointing to their guide, who was walking calmly along one of the bridges, taking her time reaching them.

"You're Sleynth?" one of the female guards asked. She was tall, with hair so blond it was nearly white.

"Yes," Queen Celina said. "My husband is King Glower the Seventy-ninth."

The guard nodded politely and said something to the male guard at her side in another language. He shrugged, and neither of them lowered their weapons.

No one moved after that until their guide reached them. She walked calmly past the guards and led them around the side of the tent to where the flaps had been tied open. Celie would have liked to stop and investigate before going into the tent, but the guards were right on the griffins' heels with their spears held crosswise, and so they let themselves be pressed forward into the dimness of the tent.

Celie hadn't realized how hot and muggy it was outside until they were inside. There were servants standing around the cloth walls with large fans, making a breeze blow through the tent. It was very refreshing. The sun had been high in the sky, but now with just lamplight shining, it was much more pleasant.

Not that Celie had much time to enjoy it. The tent was full of people, and the guards herded her and her family forward until they were right in the middle of the crowd. Everyone was sitting on low, backless stools, holding shallow bowl-like cups and sipping as they talked. Or at least Celie assumed that they'd been talking; now they were entirely silent. She liked the fact that she was taller than everyone sitting on the stools, but she didn't like the way they were all studying her.

At the far end of the tent, a wizened man with a brown face and a cloud of white hair stood up.

"You were from Sleyne?" he asked.

"Yes," Queen Celina said, stepping to the front. "We are from Sleyne. I am Queen Celina, and my husband is King Glower the Seventy-ninth." She made a little curtsy, one ruler to another. "And you are the Master of the Found?"

"Yes," he said. "I am." He sat back down. "The griffins

are new," he remarked. "How much of your ship can we salvage?"

"Salvage?" Queen Celina said, her voice faltering. "We . . . the Ship is just fine."

"Just fine?" The Master sounded as though the words didn't make sense. "You came here through the Well, did you not?"

"We did."

"Then how is your ship just fine?"

There was much murmuring among the people. Celie heard Grathian, what she was sure was Bendeswe, and even a word or two of Sleynth. Looking around the tent, she saw people of all colors and ages, all wearing the odd ribbon clothes. Or so she thought at first. Looking closer, Celie saw whole pieces of clothing that she recognized: bodices and strips of lace from Grath, the one-sleeved tunics of Bendeswe. She suspected that woven ribbons were a way of patching and mending old clothes, possibly even things that washed up on the shore after falling through the Well.

"Like the people," she whispered, looking around.

No one heard her, because all eyes were now on Queen Celina, the Master, and their guide, whose name was Kalys.

Apparently Kalys had erred by leading them directly to the City in the Trees, as this place was called. She should have gone back to the shore with Celie and Rolf and checked to see how many survivors there were and how much salvage was possible.

"They flew to the shore on *griffins*," she said in a sulky voice. "The griffins were far more interesting than how much rope we could get from their ship."

"I promise you the griffins shan't be any trouble," the queen said. "Nor will we. We need to refresh some of our supplies, and then with your help, we need to get home."

"This is your home now," the Master said, as though it were obvious. "What is found through the Well stays Found. But tell me," he went on, "how did your ship not fly into a million pieces? The force of the Well can crush a man's skull, and wood is equally brittle in its grip."

"I am a wizard," Queen Celina announced.

Since the queen was not a full wizard, she was not supposed to make such a claim. But Celie was glad that her mother had. It was much more impressive than saying that she was studying magic, and Celie had a feeling that they needed to impress the Master, immediately. Besides which, there was no one there to call her bluff.

However, the Master wasn't easy to impress. "Another wizard could be of some use," he said, much as though Queen Celina had announced that she was a shoemaker.

"I'm so very sorry," Queen Celina said. The icily formal tone of her voice would have sent anyone of the court running for cover, but the Master didn't flinch. "But I'm afraid that, since we've just come to your world from ours, we don't understand what is happening. Would you be so kind as to explain yourself?"

The Master drew himself up. He stretched out a hand, and someone put a staff into it. The staff was tipped with iron, like a Vhervhish mountain climber's walking stick, but there was a scroll wrapped around the top and tied with red thread. Lulath gave a small exclamation and whispered something to Lilah about Bendeswe.

"Before the first men fell through the Well, there was nothing here. Nothing but the land. There were fish in the ocean. There were birds in the trees. And on the land, among the trees and rocks, there were small animals, burrowing things, climbing things, small things.

"Then man began to sail the seas, and he fell into the Well. From every country of the world beyond, he sailed, and he was drawn into the Well and brought here. And so we built our cities, and we gathered the Found from every corner of the world. We gather tools. We gather cloth. We gather food. We gather what wrack and ruin comes through the Well, and we build with it." He waved his staff around, indicating the stools, the tent, the clothing, and the people. "That is what the Found are. That is what you are now.

"You have been Found."

"What an amazing thing you've done," Queen Celina said blithely. "To have built all this from the wreckage coming through the Well." She smiled around at the group. It was her court smile, the very one that Lilah had become so good at during their time in Grath. "However, I'm afraid that we cannot stay," the queen continued. "Though if there are any tools you need that we can spare from our Ship, we will happily give them to you."

"You will share all with us," the Master said. "That is what it means to be Found." He sighed. "It is not easy to be Found," he said with great sympathy.

"But we aren't Found," Queen Celina said. "Because we weren't lost."

The whole crowd of people were shaking their heads, and a few were laughing. Celie put on her own court smile, even though it wasn't half as good as her mother's. Also, she would rather have been shaking her fist at the people.

"There is no way back," the Master said, beginning to lose his patience. "The Well flows only in one direction. You are here now, and here you will stay."

Lilah slid off Juliet's back, the better to have hysterics on the floor.

"Now," the Master said, raising his voice over the howls coming from Lilah. "We will help you dismantle your ship so that you can build your homes here in the trees, away from the unicorns and other monsters."

Lilah cut off mid-sob. "Did you just say unicorns?"

Chapter 23

I can't believe you didn't tell me you saw a unicorn," Lilah ranted. She picked up a pillow from the floor, threw it across their tent, and then retrieved it so that she could sit down. "They're only the reason why we're all here."

"It tried to kill us!" Rolf protested. "We were trying to find a good way to say 'Hey, Lilah, those unicorns that you like so much are evil'!"

"And then you came, and Kalys was leading us here," Celie said. "We were in shock, and there wasn't really time."

"We've got time now," Pogue said, slumped against Arrow's side. "All the rest of our lives, apparently."

"Nonsense," Queen Celina said, rather sharply. Then she smiled—her real smile. "I mean, Pogue, darling, there's no need to be glum. The Ship brought us here for a reason,

and it's still in one piece, so that's two things in our favor."
She made a face, wrinkling her nose and bunching up her
smile. "I do wish Bran were here, or any more qualified
wizard, really, but other than that, I refuse to despair!"

"I'm sorry, Your Majesty," Pogue said. "I'll try not to . . .
despair."

"Oh, good," Rolf said. "More despair for me, then!" He
shook his head. "Mother, how do you think we're going
to get back there?" He pointed up. "*The Golden Griffin* is
amazing and magical, but even it can't fly."

"We'll sort it out," the queen said, waving a hand.

"Mummy," Celie said uneasily, "you still think this is
an adventure, don't you?"

"What else would you call it?" her mother said.

"I would call it horrible," Lilah said. "In fact, I *do* call
it horrible."

"I call it the end," Rolf added. "Just . . . the end."

"Now, this is not being talk that I am liking," Lulath
said. "Where are being my family of adventure?"

"Maybe it's because we've had one adventure too
many," Celie said. She buried her face in the soft feathers
at the base of Rufus's neck. "I just want to go *home*." And
then she embarrassed herself by bursting into tears.

"Oh, darling, darling, it will be all right," Queen
Celina said. She reclined against Rufus as well, so that
she could put her arms around Celie.

Celie felt only mildly comforted by this. They were
all going to be stuck here forever. They would live and

die in this world high above the trees, with rampaging beasts and who knew what else below. They would have to take the Ship—their beautiful Ship that they had only just built—apart to make themselves houses. It wouldn't matter much to Lilah; she and Lulath could get married just like they'd planned. But what about her, and Rolf, and Pogue? What about Daddy, and Bran, and the Castle?

"Hello," said a voice through the canvas wall of their tent. "Hello?" It sounded like Kalys. "I am coming in."

Rather than using the tent flap, she rolled under the side of the tent right by Rufus's head. He reared up, shaking off Celie and her mother, and they sat up and stared at the girl.

"Hello," she said again, and grinned at them.

"What are you doing here?" Lilah demanded.

"And why didn't you use the door?" Rolf asked. His eyes lit up. "Are you here in secret?"

"Yes," she said, nodding.

She sat up and folded her legs neatly. Then she reached up and took off her headdress. Although her skin was dark, her brown hair was a shade lighter than Lilah's or Queen Celina's, and had been braided into two braids that slithered down her back and hit the floor when she shook her head.

"Are you really from Sleyne?" she asked, setting aside her ribbon-bedecked headdress and slicking a hand over the top of her head.

"Why else would we speak Sleynth?" Lilah said tartly.

"Lilah!" Queen Celina scolded.

"I speak Sleynth, and I have never been there," Kalys said, without any hint of offense. "So you come from the Castle?" she asked Queen Celina directly. "You said that your husband is the king of the Castle? And he wears the crown and rings?" Her eyes were shining, and she was leaning forward until she almost fell over her own folded legs. She straightened herself with one hand.

"That's right," Queen Celina said.

"How do you know about the crown and rings?" Celie asked.

Kalys smoothed her braids, seemingly unaware of the shock that had just gone through the others. Celie tried to form a question, then didn't know where to start, but Kalys picked up her story once she had her hair settled.

"My people brought the unicorns here," Kalys said. "My family survived the ship from Grath that was bringing the unicorns to Larien to keep them away from the griffins, and from everyone else." She made a face.

"That's what I want to know," Lilah said. "Why do all the stories talk about the poor unicorns being hunted? We come here, and Rolf claims one tried to eat him!"

"Eat you?" Kalys looked at him in surprise. "No, no! Did I say that? No, I didn't say that!" she answered her own question. "It most certainly would not have eaten you. They don't eat people. Or animals. Just flowers. Berries." Kalys flapped her hand, a gesture not unlike one of Queen Celina's.

Lilah gave a romantic little sigh at this. "They eat flowers," she told Lulath, as though he hadn't heard.

"But it would have definitely killed you," Kalys said, oblivious to Lilah's sighs. "They see everyone and everything around them as an enemy. And they are deadly with their horns and hooves."

"Oh," Lilah said. "So, if we leave here . . . you don't think we could . . . take one back with us?"

"Definitely not," Kalys said, looking alarmed. "When they lived in Sleyne, there was no one else there, so they were safe, and others were safe from them. But now that you are there, and the griffins are there, they should *not* return. They are happy here, and the world is safer." She paused. "But when you return to Sleyne, there is one thing I would like you to take from here."

"What's that?" Rolf asked.

"Me," Kalys said. "I want you to take me."

They all sat there for a moment, stunned.

"*Can* we leave?" Lilah asked.

"What about your family?" Queen Celina said at the same time.

"You are knowing the way to the Well?" Lulath cried. "O clever!"

"Everyone knows the way to the Well," Kalys said, as though it were nothing. "But none of us have been able to get to it, because every other ship that has come through has been destroyed."

"There are enough parts here to build a fleet of ships," Pogue said, raising one eyebrow.

"Who wants to risk it?" Kalys countered. "Yours is not only the first ship to arrive whole but also the first ship that hasn't lost most of its crew. Only five people survived the ship that brought my ancestors here."

When Lilah opened her mouth, Kalys said, "Four unicorns survived."

Lilah closed her mouth, but she looked annoyed.

"Then why do you want to go with us?" Pogue asked.

Kalys put her hands up to her face and ran them over her cheeks, then up over her head and down her braids. She thought for a long time, and they all sat and watched her, waiting.

"You have griffins," she said at last. "And the Castle." She rocked back and forth on her haunches. "The Tribes are made up of people from all over the world. The other world, that is," she clarified. "There are no stories from this one. No true language. We teach each other the dances, the stories, the music, the ways from the lands we came from, in that other world. My family is called Unicorn Lost. We speak a language called Hathelocke at home—do you know it?"

"Hathelocke?" Celie recovered her voice. "None of us speak it, no, but we've been to Hatheland. And the Glorious Arkower."

"You are actually Hathelocke?" Rolf asked in amazement. "You're from Hatheland?"

Kalys closed her eyes for a moment. "I have never been there," she said when she opened them. "But I was raised to think of Hatheland as my real home, of Sleyne as my people's *new* home, and of this place as being . . . not our true home. As though we are guests."

"That's horrible," Lilah said. "To have never had a real home? I'm so sorry."

"Now I am being with friend Pogue," Lulath said. "And having to have the wonder of why you are not all building the ships and trying, trying to go to the homes."

"Most of the Found are happy here," Kalys explained. "Many of them are sailors, or their ancestors were—sailors who didn't have a connection to another land. They found this place an exciting adventure. But my family was taught that we are griffin riders in exile, and this is not our home." She tossed her head. "Some people say that we are strange and unfriendly for thinking this way. But if it's only my family, then why don't they build real houses? Or plant crops?" She looked around at them all in a challenging way.

"Which brings us to your family," Queen Celina said. "What will they do if you leave with us?"

"Nothing," Kalys said quickly, but she was looking at her hands when she said it. "My parents are dead, so I don't have a family," she added in a mutter. "And . . . well . . . there's no one."

218

"Again, so sad!" Lulath said. "I am not seeing that it is being any such problem for you to come on the mighty *Golden Griffin*! But first we must be going to the Ship, and then you must be helping us to find the Well!"

"I can do that," Kalys said. "I can help you." She hesitated. "But first . . . I just wondered . . ."

"Yes?" Queen Celina said.

She said it gently, but Celie could tell that her mother was waiting for bad news. A condition that would be impossible for them to meet. Celie certainly was expecting the worst.

"Could I touch one of the griffins?" Kalys asked wistfully.

"My dear Kalys," Rolf said in a gallant voice, "if you can get us out of here I will *give* you my griffin."

They all looked at him.

"Well, not really," he amended sheepishly. "But I mean to say, get us out of here and you can touch all the griffins you want, *including* Dagger, who is back on the Ship, which we need to get to as soon as possible."

But as soon as they walked out of the tent into the muggy open air, Rufus gave a shriek and flew off in the opposite direction from the sea, and the Ship.

"Rufus, no!" Celie shouted, as her griffin disappeared rapidly over the green treetops.

"Quick, come on," Pogue said. He held out his hand, and she took it so that he could help her onto Arrow's back.

"Our very Rufus must have seen something of impor-tance," Lulath reasoned, as he threw a long leg over Lorcan's back.

"Poor Orlath must think we're dead," Queen Celina said, looking at Juliet and Lilah. "Why don't you and I return to the Ship?"

"Dagger is probably kicking up a fuss by now," Rolf said.

"You all go back to the Ship," Pogue said. "Celie and I will catch up to Rufus."

"I have to gather some things, and then I'll find your ship," Kalys said.

Celie was keeping her eyes on the spot where Rufus had gone, much as she'd watched the white flash that had been a unicorn earlier. She was vaguely aware of some fussing about the dogs' baskets, and ended up being handed the basket with the puppies and their mother. She took it without comment, cradling it close, and finally Pogue swung onto Arrow's back behind her and they were able to take off.

"Do you trust Kalys?" Pogue said as soon as they were in the air.

"Yes," Celie said, without really thinking about it. She could no longer see Rufus, but she kept her eyes trained in the direction he'd gone. "Why shouldn't we? It won't hurt to bring her back with us. Ethan's history was even more suspicious, and that turned out well for him and us."

"True. But then why is she sneaking around, if they don't care?"

This was also true. As they passed over the village in the trees, everyone looked up, and many waved. No one seemed concerned in the slightest. They'd been told when they were taken to the private tent to rest and talk that they were free to come and go, so why had Kalys snuck in under the wall?

"Maybe she—hey!"

A gold flash had risen out of the trees and then darted back down again. Celie pointed to it, but Arrow must have also seen it, because he veered to the left and began to fly faster.

"Was that Rufus?" Pogue asked.

"No," Celie said, hope rising in her breast. "Rufus isn't that bright a gold. I think that was Lady Griffin!"

Kitsi sat up straight in the basket, raising the lid with her round head, and barked. Arrow sped up. The little dog was straining toward the place where Lady Griffin had disappeared, and Celie clutched the basket to her chest, willing Kitsi to not try to jump out before they landed.

Another flash in the trees, and this time it was Rufus, followed by his mother, and then they dove back down again. Celie's elation at finding Lady Griffin alive faltered.

"They're attacking something," Celie said.

"It looks that way," Pogue said grimly.

When they got over the spot where the other two griffins had swooped down, Arrow didn't hesitate. He folded his wings and arced between the trees, landing neatly on the moss beside Rufus. And just beyond Rufus was Lady Griffin.

"Rufus! You found your mother! Clever boy," Celie said. Pogue's arm around her waist tightened. "What? Oh."

The clearing they were standing in was a narrow corridor in the trees. They were at one end of it, and at the other end was a massive wild pig. Celie pulled the basket close to her chest, until the wicker was almost cutting through the fabric of her gown.

"Fly away," she whispered. "Rufus! Lady! Just fly!"

The pig began to charge, but Rufus and Lady Griffin screamed and flew toward it. They raked it with their talons as they flew up and over it, then dove back down, driving it back. Arrow was vibrating with the need to join them.

"Fly! Fly away!" Pogue shouted in frustration, but Arrow wouldn't listen, and neither would the others.

"I'm getting off," Celie said, sliding from Arrow's back with the basket. Kitsi and her puppies had gone mad, barking and rattling the basket.

The pig made another charge, and Celie screamed and sank to the ground, curling around the basket, but the griffins beat the pig back again. Pogue leaped from Arrow's back, allowing his griffin to join the others, and drew his sword. He stood between Celie and the fight, moaning that he needed a spear, not a sword.

"What are they *doing?*" Celie cried. "Are they trying to actually kill it?" She had never seen Rufus hunt anything other than a stuffed toy.

"I don't know," Pogue said, frustrated. He made some lunges toward the pig, shouting and brandishing his sword. "Hah! Hah!"

"Why won't it leave?" Celie said. "Ouch!"

Kitsi had flipped open the lid of the basket with her head, and it hit Celie in the chin, making her bite her tongue. The little dog tumbled out and onto the moss. Celie tried to grab her with one hand while holding the basket of puppies with the other, but the dog eluded her and went to a large fern right where Rufus had just landed.

Celie felt all the blood drain from her face.

"Kitsi," she whispered, her mouth dry. "Kitsi, please come!"

Kitsi had begun to dig as though she'd smelled a treat hidden in the ferns. With Pogue guarding her, Celie crept closer, one eye on the dog and the other on the wild pig.

Suddenly Kitsi's barks were answered by a high-pitched whinny from within the fern. The sound drove the wild pig to absolute madness, and it let out a truly hair-raising squeal as it charged straight for the fern, the dog, and Celie.

Pogue leaped forward and braced himself with his sword point extended. All three griffins leaped. There

223

was a horrible sound of screams, and Celie squeezed her eyes shut and prepared for the worst.

Silence.

She opened her eyes and saw Rufus and Arrow, triumphant, standing over the dead pig.

"I think I'm going to be sick," Celie said.

"Why? You're safe now," Kalys said, dropping down from the trees.

"Thank you for your help," Pogue said wryly.

"I only just got here," she said, contrite. Then she spread her hands. "And I have no weapon. I would only have been in the way!

"Now let's see what the fuss was about."

She knelt beside Celie and parted the ferns. In a hollow at the base of a tree, hidden by the green leaves of the underbrush, was a delicate baby unicorn.

Chapter
24

It looked at them with wide, frightened eyes and whinnied pitifully.

"The pig probably killed the mother," Kalys said.

As if it understood what she'd just said, the baby bleated and hid its face, with its tiny nub of a horn, under one gangly foreleg. Lady Griffin, too, seemed to understand, and she came to stand guard over the baby, pushing Kalys aside with a wing. The queen griffin gave Celie a speaking look.

"We're taking the baby unicorn with us?" Celie asked. "But they . . . they fight and are horrible!"

"Not if you can get them this young," Kalys said.

"What?" Celie sat back on her heels. "What about all that talk of them being dangerous and killing things and people?"

Kalys gestured to the pig. "Some people keep pigs as pets, but wild pigs are killers," she said reasonably. "The trouble with unicorns is that it's impossible to get a baby and raise it to be tame, because the parents won't let you anywhere near. But they're smart. After all, my ancestors managed to herd them across three countries and onto a ship, and keep them alive for weeks at sea. If they were mindless killers, that wouldn't have been possible."

"So you really think if we took this baby, Lilah could raise it to be tame?" Pogue said.

"Hey," Celie interrupted. "Maybe *I* want to raise it."

"I assumed that you had more common sense," Pogue said.

Celie burst out laughing. "Actually, you're right; I don't want it. But Lilah will!"

Recognizing that she was about to get her way, Lady Griffin stepped back. Celie carefully gathered up the baby unicorn, and Kalys helped her tie it over Rufus's back with ribbons unraveled from the hem of her skirt.

Kalys worked with surprising dexterity. She seemed to know exactly where to tie the unicorn's legs so that they wouldn't interfere with Rufus's wings, and positioned the little unicorn so that Celie could sit behind it. Then she very reverently stroked Rufus's head, after looking to Celie for permission.

"How did you know how to do that?" Celie asked.

"I told you. My family is trained to be griffin riders. Even though we thought there were no more griffins, we still pass down that knowledge. I know all about caring for griffins." She made a face. "And I'm the first person in a dozen generations of my family to see one." She tried to run a hand over her hair but she was wearing her head-dress, so instead she just adjusted the ribbons hanging around her face.

"Would the rest of your family like to see the griffins before we go?" Celie asked. "I'm sure we could stop and tell them good-bye."

Pogue flashed her a look as he mounted Arrow. Celie watched Kalys's face carefully as she answered.

"I don't have any more family," she said firmly. "They have all passed on. I am the last person to come from Hatheland."

"Oh," Celie said, reassured. She could see that Kalys was telling the truth.

"And that's why I have to leave," Kalys said.

She closed her eyes and took several deep breaths. Pogue and Celie exchanged looks, but waited for her to speak. Celie knew they were about to get the rest of the truth.

"The Master has decided that it's time for me to marry into a Found family," Kalys said. "Since there are none of the Unicorn Lost left, they wish me to marry into the Griffin Lost."

"The Griffin Lost?" Celie said. "But . . . is that what they call us?"

"How would they have decided that so quickly?" Pogue asked, looking equally baffled.

"The Griffin Lost," Kalys said, shaking her head, "are those who lost the griffins." She gave them a meaningful look, but they could only stare back. "The Arkish."

"There are Arkish here?" Celie said so loudly that the baby unicorn bleated and Kitsi barked.

Pogue and Celie exchanged another look. "When did they get here?" he asked. "Are any of them wizards?"

Kalys looked startled by their reaction and hurried to explain. "No, no wizards. They only came last year. They have been living in some other place, since they left the Glorious Arkower, along with my people." She made a face. "They do not say much; they keep to themselves. But they have agreed that I may marry among them if I never speak Hathelocke again, or mention griffins or the Castle."

Pogue rocked back on his heels. "Looks like we've found the missing village," he said. "And we were right: they're Arkish."

"Why didn't you say so before?" Celie said to Kalys. "That's awful! We can't let that happen!"

"Right," Pogue said. "You'd better come with us."

He handed Celie the basket of dogs, with Kitsi once more inside, and she balanced it in front of her on the baby unicorn's back. He held out an arm to Kalys and swung her up behind him on Arrow. Kalys couldn't help laughing from sheer joy, and that made Pogue and Celie smile as well. They set off for the Ship, with Lady Griffin leading the way.

"Can I get my things?" Kalys called to Celie as they rose above the crown of the trees.

"Of course," Celie called back.

Kalys directed them to a spot that looked like any other part of the jungle. But when Arrow and then Rufus dipped down into the trees, they saw a series of brightly colored tents hidden among the branches—like the City in the Trees, but on a much smaller scale. The trees themselves were so close together that several of the bridges between them were doors laid flat, with woven ropes as handrails.

They landed on the wooden terrace of one of the tents, though they weren't really tents, Celie saw on closer inspection. Most of them were wooden houses, up to about waist height. But there the builders appeared to have run out of wood, and from the middle of each wall up to the roof the houses were made of sailcloth. Everything was much more worn than in the City in the Trees, and there were dead leaves in the corners of the terrace.

Kalys saw where Celie was looking and made a face.

"It's hard to take care of it all by myself," she said defensively.

"By yourself?" Pogue said, looking around curiously.

From where they were standing, they could see five or six of the half-wooden, half-canvas houses, all linked by short bridges. But there were no signs of any people, and some of the houses were badly in need of repair. Drifted leaves were nothing compared to the rips in the canvas Celie saw, and in one place, a tree branch had fallen and was sticking out haphazardly from a cloth roof.

"What is this place?" Celie asked.

"It's my home," Kalys said, still sounding defensive. "I told you: I'm the only one left."

"You live here alone?" Pogue asked in surprise.

Celie, embarrassed, fiddled with the ribbons tying the unicorn to Rufus. Improbably, the little creature had gone to sleep. She supposed it had been a very long day for the unicorn. It had been a very long day for Celie as well.

But Kalys had climbed off Arrow's back and was leading them into her home. Celie slipped down from Rufus's harness, tucking the basket of dogs under one arm and leading her griffin with the other.

Inside it was clean and tidy and looked like the main room of any cottage Celie had ever seen. There was a small round table, though there were cushions to sit on instead of chairs, and the table was very low. The pots and plates were displayed on shelves above a small cooking stove that was cobbled together from mismatched pieces, but was shiny and clean all the same. There were a couple of trunks, and slung along the back wall was a hammock like the kind the sailors on *The Golden Griffin* slept in, except it was woven of red and pink strips rather than white canvas. That was Kalys's bed, Celie realized with a shock. She wondered if the other girl had ever slept on a mattress with a pillow, but knew it would be rude to ask.

"It will only take me a moment," Kalys said.

Kalys opened one of the trunks and pulled out an armload of clothing. She threw it into the hammock. She took a picture off the wall, a painting of a family, and put it in atop the clothes with considerably more care. Then she put some small carvings into the hammock and took it off the wall, deftly wrapping the hammock around the clothes, picture, and carvings and making it into a bundle she could carry. She took some long strips of cloth out of the bottom of the trunk and used them to make straps so that she could put the whole bundle on her back. Then she turned to go.

"I'm ready," she said calmly, though her eyes looked shiny with unshed tears.

"We—we have room on the Ship," Pogue said. "You could bring more things. We could carry your trunks between the griffins or something."

"Yes," Celie said hastily, feeling bad that she hadn't thought to say something sooner. "And . . . and . . . I'm sorry, but did you really live here all by yourself?" she blurted out.

"Yes," Kalys said. "But only since . . . only since my parents died."

"So all this was just for your family?" Celie asked, pointing out the window to the abandoned tree houses nearby.

"Oh, no," Kalys said. "These were the homes of all the Unicorn Lost."

"There are a lot of houses," Pogue observed, looking out another window.

"There were five households, originally," Kalys said. "Then there grew to be as many as twelve, for a time." She shrugged again. "There were but two when I was a child, and now there is only me."

"What happened to them?" Celie couldn't help but ask, though she quickly added, "I mean, if you want to talk about it."

"It's all right." Kalys looked surprised at Celie's question. "It just . . . happens, you know? Fevers, falls, that sort of thing."

Pogue and Celie could only look at her, and then at each other. There had been twelve households; how many were in a household? And now they were all gone? That seemed like an awful lot of fevers, falls, and "that sort of thing" to Celie, and she could see that Pogue felt the same.

"I'm ready," Kalys said.

She adjusted her pack on her back. It was very small.

"You can bring more," Pogue told her again.

"None of this is mine," she said, waving a hand at the rest of the house.

"But you said this is your house," Celie said.

"It is, or it was," Kalys said. She pursed her lips as though looking for the right words. "It was my house when I needed a house to live in," she said at last. "And those were the pots we cooked in, the dishes we ate from," she explained as she pointed to the dresser. "But now others here who need them will take them. Because I'm guessing you have pots of your own."

"Well, yes," Pogue said, frowning. "But—"

"We have pots," Celie said firmly. "We have trunks and dressers. Beds and blankets." She nodded her head decisively. "You'll like sleeping in a proper bed. And it will be *your* bed. Your own . . . things."

"That will be strange," Kalys said. "But I think it might be good strange."

"I think so, too," Celie said. "Better than living by yourself."

She couldn't believe that Kalys, who was probably only fifteen years old, had been left to live on her own! Her parents had died, and these "Found" people had just ignored her, let her take care of a whole cluster of houses alone? Celie didn't like that idea at all. The empty tree houses reminded her of Hatheland, and the abandoned stables and ruined courtyard of the Castle that had been left behind. It had been so lonely there, even with her brother and sister and Pogue and Lulath with them. She couldn't imagine what it was like for Kalys to actually be alone in this house, so high above the ground and so far from the center of the city.

They went back out of the tree house, and Kalys latched the door very carefully. There was no lock, but Celie supposed that if everything was shared, and nothing really belonged to anyone except the clothes one was wearing, no one would steal. And if they did steal something, where would they go? Looking down off the edge of the platform made Celie feel sick; they were so high up! And looking out over the treetops she could see the roofs of other houses, but beyond them there was nothing.

They climbed back onto the griffins, and once again the little unicorn woke up. It bleated a bit, but Celie stroked it quiet again, and it went back to sleep. It seemed awfully young, and Celie hoped they would be able to find something for it to eat. It would be awful to come all this way and then have the little creature sicken on the way home because they couldn't take care of it well enough.

Chapter
25

They were almost past the City in the Trees when the puppies, tired of being trapped in a basket, began to wrestle. The basket leaped and writhed, and then Celie felt it slip out of her sweaty palms.

"No!" she screamed as it fell.

Lady Griffin dove after it and almost caught it. Her fumbling talons knocked it to the side, and it landed atop one of the tents. The basket hit the canvas and exploded open, and Kitsi and her puppies all slithered out and rolled down the sloping roof and off the side of the tent.

Rufus landed on the tent's platform without any guidance from Celie, who was busy uselessly shouting Kitsi's name. She kicked Kalys by accident in getting off Rufus's back, and then tripped over the hem of her own gown. Kalys helped her up and then guided her around the side of the tent. There, on a wooden ledge no more than a pace wide, was a rather surprised-looking weaver holding a basket of ribbons with three of the puppies in it. On the platform by her feet were Kitsi and the other puppy, looking slightly stunned but none the worse for wear.

"Oh, thank goodness, thank goodness," Celie said, tears springing to her eyes.

"They fell right into my basket," the weaver said in Grathian with a delighted laugh. "Wasn't that lucky?"

"That was amazing; you're amazing," Celie babbled in the same language. "They fell right out of my hands. But you saved them!"

The woman blushed. "It was nothing! I'm sure they would have been fine if I hadn't caught them! Look at little mother; she's all right."

Indeed, Kitsi had shaken herself thoroughly and was now busy alternately licking the puppy by her side and standing on her hind legs to try to see the ones in the basket. The weaver put the basket down and reunited the little family.

"Celie? I'm afraid to look," Pogue called from around the corner of the tent.

"They're fine," Celie called back. "Someone caught them."

Pogue made a noise that sounded like he was choking on a laugh and a sigh at the same time. "Well," he said a moment later. "Hurry and get them, because people are coming."

The original basket had caught on the top of the tent, and the weaver offered them her own. She dumped out the cloth she was carrying—bits and pieces that she was going to weave into the ribbony fabric they all wore—into a larger canvas bag and gave the basket to Celie. Celie coaxed the dogs inside, where they were only too happy to go, having been duly chastened by their fall. The only trouble was that the new basket didn't have a lid, and Celie wondered if they should tie the puppies to the basket, and then the basket to Rufus's harness.

By that time, the Master and one his guards had found them. He looked at the griffins, the baby unicorn, Kalys, Pogue, Celie, and the dogs, and then he shook his head.

"Come and speak to me," he entreated Kalys.

Kalys sighed. Pogue and Celie shrugged. Kalys took the basket of puppies and shuffled after the Master while Celie and Pogue flew the griffins to his tent. There were only a handful of people inside: his guards, and a middle-aged man who began to berate Kalys in a vaguely familiar language while a younger man looked on with a smug expression.

"Are you the one she's supposed to marry?" Celie asked the young man in Grathian, interrupting his father.

They both looked surprised that she would even talk to them. Or maybe that she spoke Grathian. Then the young man nodded.

237

"We are to marry in ten days," he said sullenly, in near perfect Grathian.

This confirmed Celie's suspicion that while that griffin rider village in Grath hadn't let anyone learn their language or even where they had come from, they had been spying on their neighbors all along.

"She doesn't want to marry you," Celie said. "She doesn't want to give up being a Hathelocke and become Arkish."

The older man looked outraged, but Celie went on regardless.

"She wants to leave, so we're taking her with us."

Celie wanted to leave. The humid heat was making her head feel heavy, and she was sticky all over. She wanted to be back on the Ship, headed home. She did not want to have to stand, sweating, while this obnoxious boy got his father to yell at Kalys for him.

"Of course we're taking her with us," Queen Celina said, coming into the Master's tent. Orlath was with her, and Lulath and Lilah. "We wondered what was taking so long, so we—" She stopped short. "Is that—"

"Look, Lilah," Celie said. "We found you a unicorn!"

"What?" Lilah ran forward to see the little creature, still wide awake and protesting its captivity. She stopped just before she touched it. "But is it dangerous?" She looked torn between finally touching a unicorn and getting bitten by it.

"That is the other thing I wished to speak to you about," the Master said. "And yes, please, the beast is in distress." He gestured for Lilah to untie the unicorn.

She quickly began to undo the ribbons, and Kalys helped her.

"If you will raise it and train it properly, it will be like your griffins," the old man said. "Deadly to enemies, gentle to friends. It is rare for a unicorn to be tamed, but it can be done," he assured Queen Celina.

"But you don't want us to take him, do you?" she asked shrewdly.

"Her—it's a her!" Lilah corrected their mother with delight.

She sank to the floor and pulled the unicorn's head onto her lap, cooing and clucking. Celie watched anxiously, especially when Juliet approached. But Juliet, after sniffing the unicorn over thoroughly, sank down beside Lilah and looked on, unconcerned.

"I don't believe you will make it back through the Well," he said bluntly. "I don't think that Kalys, in wanting to leave this place, has been honest."

Celie quickly explained to her mother why Kalys wanted to leave. Kalys's intended kept interrupting, as did his father, to insist that she was being childish and that she belonged with them, but the Glowers and the Master ignored them. Celie could tell by the look on the Master's face whenever the Arkish spoke that they hadn't exactly made friends in the City in the Trees during their time there.

"If Kalys is willing to make the journey, we will take her with us," Queen Celina said. She fixed a frosty eye on the angry suitor and his father. "Where we come from, we don't force girls to marry against their will."

"We don't, either," the Master said, holding up his hands in a conciliatory gesture. "But we require all of our people to have a place, and to be useful," he explained. "We have so little here. Every person, every item that we can salvage is precious. We strive to preserve customs, languages, and the ways of every people who come to us through the Well, but they must also add to our society."

"I understand," Queen Celina said.

"There is no need for a griffin trainer here, without griffins," the Master went on. "Nor do we need the Hathelocke language to be taught to our children, since Kalys alone speaks it now. It is for Kalys to change her ways, if she wishes to remain here."

"But I don't wish to remain here," Kalys said passionately.

"Then you may go," the Master agreed sadly. "Though I think it might be to your death."

The Arkish intended and his father began shouting, but one of the guards escorted them out without even waiting for a signal from the Master. Everyone breathed a sigh of relief when they were gone, not just Kalys.

The Master looked at the small pack on Kalys's back. "But what do you have there?" he asked.

Kalys flushed. "They are my things," she said angrily.

"Can they be used for the good of the Found?" The Master's voice was fatherly and gentle, but Celie wanted to grab Kalys and run out the door with her. Especially when Kalys, near tears, unfolded her makeshift hammock-pack and showed her meager belongings to the room.

"That is well," the Master said. "There is no use for the picture. And each person is allowed two suits of clothing and their own bedding," he told Queen Celina proudly.

"I understand that life is hard for you here," the queen said politely. "If we dared to spare supplies from our Ship, we would surely do so. I *can* offer you some lovely blue cloth, recently purchased in NeiMai, as a gift in return for allowing us to take Kalys with us."

"I'll go get it," Pogue offered.

"Wait just a moment," Lilah said, looking up from her adoring contemplation of the unicorn. "Are you saying that all you own in the world is that little bundle?"

"Yes," Kalys said, and her dark cheeks flushed.

"You don't have a home?" Lilah demanded, and Lulath made a soft exclamation of sympathy.

"I do!" Kalys said. "I mean, I *did*. The griffin riders, we had houses, but now—"

"Those houses will be used by people who need them," the Master explained. "And Kalys was to marry into another family and be a useful member of their household." He paused. "I know that before, your people were rivals," he told Kalys. "But here we cannot have fighting amongst the Found. And the Arkish and the Hathelocks, as you were once called, have much in common. The match would make much more sense than marrying you into one of the sailing clans, say."

"I see," Lilah said, arching one eyebrow.

"We cannot survive unless everyone contributes, unless everyone does their part," the Master went on.

"So Kalys was expected to contribute to that other family, but now she won't?" Rolf said. "I say—is that a problem if she goes with us?"

They all looked at him, Kalys ever more red-faced and humiliated.

"I want her to come with us, but—" Rolf said, but then he broke off, red in the face as well.

Lulath patted his shoulder, then Kalys's shoulder. He was uncharacteristically quiet, and Celie could see that the tall prince was thinking hard about something.

"She will come us," Lilah declared. "She will be more useful to us than she is here. We need her. We need someone who knows about Hatheland, and who speaks Hathelocke, to help us with our griffins. And someone who knows about unicorns."

"I have heard the stories of such people," the Master said musingly. "And how they take and take, but now I see it plain before me."

"You take from the Well," Celie interjected hotly.

"Are you saying that we're taking too much?" Lilah asked a moment later, before the Master could even begin to argue with Celie.

Lilah had the bargaining look on her face, the one that she'd had when they'd been in NeiMai. She was on her feet, and the little unicorn began to chew on her skirt, but Lilah didn't look down. Her eyes were on the Master.

"Well, then, that's easy enough: you may keep this unicorn, but we are definitely taking Kalys." She twitched her skirt out of the unicorn's mouth, and it gave a little cry. Lilah's face tightened, but she still didn't take her eyes off the Master.

"My Lilah!" Lulath exclaimed.

"You are a young woman of great nobility," the Master said admiringly. "It is a shame that you will not stay." He waved a hand. "Kalys may go with you, by her own choice, of course. And we have no use for the unicorn, so fear not, you may take it as well."

"Thank you," Lilah said, looking pleased with herself. She sat down and pulled the little unicorn back into her lap.

They all looked at Lilah for a moment—even the Master—with expressions of varying degrees of shock and admiration. Kalys sat down on the floor by Lilah and briefly rested her forehead on the older girl's shoulder. Lilah gently patted Kalys's hand and went back to stroking the unicorn.

"Well," Queen Celina murmured, "that gives me one less child to worry about."

"Are you worried about me?" Celie asked, indignant.

"Only when you climb onto roofs," her mother said.

Looking astonished at Lilah's behavior, Pogue left for the Ship to fetch the blue cloth. As they waited for him to return, one of the guards came to speak to them. It was the tall woman.

"Master," she said politely, "should we give them the other unicorn?"

"What?" Lilah jerked her head around to stare at the guard. "There's another one? A tame one?" She gave the Master a narrow look.

"Yes; my brother and I found the mother a few weeks ago," the guard said. "She was tangled in the sticking vines by the river, and had injured herself trying to break free. We sadly had to end her suffering, but then we discovered that she had a youngling, a male. He was nearby, also stuck in the vines, but him we were able to rescue. We thought to care for him until he could live on his own, but . . ." She pointed with her spear to Lilah. "If you are to take a female, you should have a male. She would be the last of her kind in your land all over again."

The Master sighed heavily. "Another thing taken from us," he said.

"But there is being something given in return," Lulath

244

said. "A several things, which will be of more joy than this unicorn."

"The fabric is a noble gift," the Master said grudgingly. "Whole cloth is rare." He fingered his cloak of woven ribbons.

"And these fine small dogs are also being noble gifts," Lulath said, standing up and pointing to the basket Celie was holding on her knees.

"What?" Celie said, rather too loudly. It startled one of the puppies, which fell out and began to cheep in distress.

"Lulath, no!" Lilah protested. She handed the unicorn to Kalys and got to her feet beside him. "You can't!"

"They're too young," Queen Celina said.

"But of course the proud mother must stay," Lulath said. His voice thickened as he said it. "My Kitsi is such the good and happy mother," he told the female guard.

She put down her spear and went to Lulath. She put a hand on his shoulder. "My name is Seren," she said. "Thank you for this noble gift." Then she walked over to Celie, squatted down, and held out a hand. Kitsi licked it, wagging her tail, and then began dropping puppies out of the basket, displaying them with obvious pride.

"With my Lorcan, the caring for the small dogs is more the hardest to remember," Lulath said. "Here it is my thinking that they are having attention all to themselves." He bent down and stroked Kitsi, and then each of her puppies. "Her name is being Kitsi, but we are having no names for these her babies."

"We will give them good names, and good homes," Seren said. "And, while there aren't dogs such as this here, there are other fine breeds, and we will find good mates for them when they are older."

"Ah, so fine," Lulath said.

A tear ran down his nose and dripped on one of the puppies, and he wiped it off. Seren put an arm around Lulath's shoulders and gave him a quick hug.

Pogue returned. "What's happening? Did they get hurt when they fell?"

"They fell?" Lilah asked. She had also put her arms around Lulath, and now she looked up, concerned.

"No, no," Celie said, choking back tears of her own. "It's not that." She sucked in a deep breath and wiped her face on her sleeve. "In exchange for a male unicorn, Lulath has offered to leave Kitsi and her puppies here," she said.

"Oh," Pogue said. He stopped unstrapping the fabric from Arrow's back. "Oh, Lulath, that's so generous of you." He patted Lulath on the back.

"Well, will that do?" Queen Celina asked the Master tartly. "Here is some fine cloth, and some of the most prized dogs in the kingdom of Grath!"

"These are generous gifts indeed," Seren said. She picked up one of the puppies and put it to her shoulder like a baby. "More than generous!" She grinned as the puppy licked her ear. "We are in your debt!"

The Master gave her a dirty look. "They are fine gifts," he said stiffly.

"May we leave, then?" Queen Celina was angry, and there was no painted-on court smile anymore. "Or will you take a moment to explain to us why this journey is so dangerous?"

The Master was offended by her tone, and he drew himself up to his full height, which made him roughly an inch taller than Celie.

"The entrance to the Well in this world is not far, but you must sail through sharp rocks to get to it. Then you must survive the crushing pull of the Well all over again. Do you really think you will be so lucky twice?" He shook his head. "No one is so lucky! You should stay with us. Your crew, your ship, your griffins. Stay."

"It wasn't luck," Queen Celina said.

"It was magic," Lilah said.

"And the Ship," Celie added.

"Thank you for your hospitality," Rolf said, bowing. "And now, we're leaving."

Chapter
26

⟨⁓⟩

It was dusk and they were all starving by the time they got on board the Ship. Celie collapsed to the deck, falling off Rufus's back and lying on her face on the still-warm boards. She thought she was being a bit dramatic, but then she looked over and saw Lilah and Lulath sitting nearby, their hands pressed to the deck, and she didn't feel overly emotional. It felt wonderful to be back on the Ship, and she liked to think the Ship had cheered up, too.

Kalys wasted no time in positioning herself at the helm with Orlath, to guide him to the Well. Lilah and Lulath sat on the deck near Celie to fuss over the baby unicorns, and Celie was about to close her eyes when a platter arrayed with slices of apples and cheese was laid in front of her.

"We did it, Cel," Rolf said, sitting down and helping himself to the food. "We survived another adventure."

"No, we haven't," she corrected him. "Not yet." Still lying down, she swiped a slice of cheese and sandwiched it between two pieces of apple. No sense dying on an empty stomach. "We still have to make it back through the Well."

"We will," Rolf said easily. "Look how happy the Ship is about it."

It was true. The Ship had come about with impressive speed. The sails and ropes snapped in the breeze in a merry way, and the men of the crew were whistling as they went about their business, catching the mood of the Ship.

"Oh, Celie," Lilah said, scuttling closer on her rear with the smaller unicorn still on her lap. "I can't believe it! We did it! *Two* unicorns!"

Lulath was holding the other unicorn, which was indeed male. It was slightly larger and had a peach-tinted coat. Its horn was twice as long as the tiny female's, but like hers it was rounded on the top, not the deadly weapon the adults sported. Celie wondered when it would get sharp, and how hard it was going to be to teach the unicorns not to hurt people with their horns.

She supposed they would just have to apply the same teaching methods they had used to train the griffins not to eat small dogs, and the small dogs not to chew on the furniture. As she thought this, JouJou came to her to be petted, and she noticed Arrow standing at attention just behind Pogue. Celie relaxed slightly. It could be done. If dogs and griffins could be trained, unicorns could be trained, she decided.

"But, Lulath," Celie said, finally sitting up. "Poor Lulath!"

He looked over at her and smiled. "Could I deny my Lilah a unicorn, when she had come so far for one?" he said softly in Grathian. His smile widened. "And now, along with still having many fine dogs—and griffins—we are the only people with pet unicorns in the world." He ruffled the little beast's soft mane. "My mother will die of envy!"

Celie had to laugh at that.

Hearing her, Queen Celina came bustling over. "Have you all eaten? Because we need to get ready," she said.

"Get ready for what?" Rolf said around a mouthful of food.

Celie hurried to get her share. Rolf was very competitive in his eating, and if you wanted anything, you had to grab it quick. One of the cook's boys had also brought some meat for Rufus, and she thanked him. He gave her a worried look, and Celie couldn't muster any reassuring words for him.

"You take this," Queen Celina said to Celie, handing her the end of a piece of string with a blob of blue wax on it, "and walk around the mast sun-wise." She handed the other end to Rolf. "You take this and go the other way.

"My protection spell did very nicely coming through the Well," the queen went on, speaking loudly so that all the crew nearby could hear. "But I thought we could be better prepared for next time, with a more specific spell."

The crew visibly relaxed, and the boy who had brought the griffins food gave a weak cheer. Celie and Rolf took their string and walked around the mast, crossing past each other three times, as though they were dancing around a maypole. Lilah and Lulath, their hands full with what to feed their new pets, went below to secure the unicorns and the remaining dogs in Lulath's cabin, and to figure out what to feed the unicorns.

Once Rolf and Celie were done, Queen Celina wrote some things with chalk on the base of the mast. Then she went to the bow and the helm to do the same. Celie followed her, out of curiosity, but none of the things her mother was doing made any sense to her. She stayed at the helm with Orlath and Pogue, because from the after deck and the helm she could get a better view of the ring of black rocks that they were approaching.

"That's where the Well is here," Kalys told her. "Inside the stones."

"How do we get the Ship past the stones?" Celie said.

"There's an opening to the south," Kalys said. "And this clever ship seems to know exactly where!" She stroked the rail near the wheel fondly.

"If you think the Ship is clever, you just wait until you get to the Castle," Rolf said, joining them.

"I can't wait," Kalys said, turning away from Rolf as though suddenly shy.

And that's when Celie knew. The Ship hadn't brought them through the Well to get unicorns. It had brought them through the Well to get Kalys.

The last of her people. The last of the griffin riders of Hatheland. And now they would take her back to the Castle—the Castle where her ancestors had lived long before Celie's. Celie wondered how long the Castle would wait before locking Kalys and Rolf in the throne room together. She turned to study the ring of black rocks rising out of the sea, not sure how she felt about that.

There wasn't much time to worry about Rolf and Kalys and what the Castle would think of her, though. The rocks were coming up fast. Orlath guided the wheel with just one hand, as the Ship did indeed seem to know what to do.

But as they got closer to the narrow break in the rocks, Celie began to feel less and less sure about the cleverness of the Ship. The water within the ring wasn't just swirling the way it had in their world, but churning greenish-white with geysers erupting along the edge, shooting water as high as the jagged rocks, which were themselves as sharp as spears and easily as tall as the Ship.

"Orlath," Celie said. "Do you think we—"

She was interrupted by a small dog hurling itself at her

legs. Which was fine, because she really didn't know what she was going to say. And because it was JouJou, who was Celie's favorite. Also, because JouJou was very upset.

Celie decided not to finish her question. Instead she picked up the little dog and held her close, letting JouJou lick her chin and wriggle.

"O our Celie! You have got her, the naughty!" Lulath said, coming above deck. "She is not liking the new tiny unicorn companions," he said, and patted JouJou's head. "Will you be holding her for this, the new adventure?"

"Oh, yes," Celie said. "I can do that. But are you staying below? Will you take Rufus down?" She peered over the edge of the rail, but there was no sign of any of the griffins. "Oh, no!"

"Not to be worrying, my our Celie," Lulath said. "That magnificent Lady Griffin, she is taking all the griffins below. I am thinking if you will be going below deck, you will not be finding room for you. They are, every golden darling, in the cabin of yours."

"Oh, good!" Celie said. "Perfect, actually."

"And you and JouJou will come here with me," Queen Celina said. "Lulath, you're going below?"

Lulath said he was, and the queen told him to take Kalys and Rolf with him. They both protested, but she ordered them to go and they went, grumbling. Celie braced herself to argue to stay on deck herself, but her mother just shook her head.

"I have a terrible feeling that if I try to make you go below, you'll sneak out again, which is probably more dangerous," she said.

Celie sheepishly kissed the silky top of JouJou's little round head.

"Just as I thought," her mother said. "And, Pogue, I don't have any right to order you to do anything, unless I draw upon my queenly rank. But I hate to do that. And I think Orlath could probably use another pair of hands anyway."

"Yes, Your Majesty," Pogue said, and bowed before he went to the helm.

"So, you," Queen Celina said to Celie, "come with me!"

They made their way to the bow, where her mother made her sit on the deck so that the rail protected her. Then she sat beside Celie and gathered her in her arms. They were soon soaked as the spray from the rocks showered down on the Ship. Looking through the rail, Celie could see the black rocks on either side of them. They were close enough to touch, and a quick glance aft showed her that Pogue and Orlath were both involved in guiding the ship, to make sure they didn't put a hole in the hull as they passed through.

Then they were through the rocks and into the bubbling cauldron of the Well.

The Ship began to spin, and nothing the crew or Pogue or Orlath could do would stop it. It dipped and spun, and the water frothed and spouted. Celie wished with all her heart that she'd gone below, but there was nothing she could do now. She was afraid to move. Celie clutched Jou-Jou tight, and Queen Celina clutched Celie, and then . . .

The blackness swallowed them.

The force of the water and the sound was so intense that it became nothingness. Celie's ears simply couldn't hear it anymore, and her mind couldn't comprehend what was happening. She wasn't sure if she was breathing air or water or nothing at all. She wasn't sure if she was floating or still sitting firmly on the deck. There was just . . . nothing.

And then it was over.

Chapter
27

"We're almost there," Lilah called to Celie.

Celie nodded broadly so that Lilah could see. They were on their griffins, flying north, high above the road where the coaches and wagons rumbled along. Celie didn't need to be told that they were close. She had flown over this same stretch of road and these same fields many times.

Up ahead, just beyond a hump of hills and down in the valley, lay the Castle.

But even being in familiar country was hard for Celie. She wanted to be home. Now. They had been gone too long.

It had taken two months to sail back to Grath from the Well. Everyone had survived, but the Ship had been damaged, and they'd had to make repairs as they sailed north. The top of the mast had broken off, and they'd strapped a spar to it to hold up the mainsail. There had been a hole in the hull that had to be patched immediately. Several of the crew had been injured, and Rolf had fallen and broken his right arm.

When they'd limped back into the harbor in Grath, they could hear the cheers and shouts from the dock. By the time they tied up at the dock, the king and queen were there with the entire court. Queen Amatopeia had been unable to speak, had only wept with joy and clung to each of them in turn. Much to everyone's surprise, Queen Celina had also burst into tears, and the two queens had stood on the dock for ages, sobbing into each other's arms.

Because they hadn't dared to stop again at the Neira Isles—not now that they had griffins *and* unicorns—they'd had to buy supplies off passing ships that had some to spare. Some of those ships had been Grathian courier ships, the fastest vessels at sea, now that *The Golden Griffin* was damaged. The couriers had carried word straight to Grath that the Ship was on its way back to port, with everyone safe and sound, even though they'd been through the Well and back. Standing on the dock, surrounded by animals and overwrought Grathian courtiers, Celie realized that they'd been presumed dead months ago, and that the news that they'd been through the Well had been both miraculous and the realization of the king and queen's worst fears.

The land had moved disturbingly under her feet after so many days at sea. Seeing this, King Kurlath had picked up

Celie and Lilah as though they were children and placed them in the coach to return to the Sanctuary, kissing each of them on the cheek once again as he did so. They had even brought a wagon for the griffins, and so Rufus and his fellows and the unicorns had ridden in comfort behind the royal entourage back to the Sanctuary.

But they hadn't stayed in the Sanctuary for long. All of them were anxious to get back to Sleyne. When the Ship had first sailed away, with no sign of ever turning back, King Kurlath had sent the news to King Glower. Celie's father had been beside himself, and Bran had come to the Sanctuary to see if he could use magic to track them across the water. Failing, he'd been invited to stay, but had hurried back to the Castle to be with King Glower, both of them now worrying that they were the only members of the family left.

Rufus was soaring over the trees that covered the hills that cupped the valley. After so long on the Ship, all of them had gotten out of shape, and the griffins grew winded during very short flights, so they'd been practicing. As they'd traveled, they'd taken all the griffins— even Dagger—on longer and longer flights. Dagger was big enough for Rolf to ride now, though not for very long.

But Rufus, the oldest of the griffins except for his mother, had no trouble flying the distance to the Castle that lay ahead of them. Any other day Celie would have guided him down to the wagons to rest after so long a flight, but not today. Rufus sensed it, too, and he just kept going as she urged him on. Lilah and Juliet had dropped back, but Celie didn't bother to look and see if they had gone to the wagons or were just flying much slower. She saw a flash of gold out of the corner of her eye and turned to the other side to see Lady Griffin keeping pace with them. Celie grinned and crouched lower on Rufus's back, putting her face against his neck.

"Go home, boy; go home," she called to him.

Rufus sped through the lowering sun, the wind streaking over them.

They crested the rise of the hills, and then they were down in the valley. Ahead of them lay the village, with the school where Queen Celina often went to tell the children stories, and Pogue's father's blacksmith shop. Tears were streaming from Celie's eyes as they passed over the village, but whether it was the wind or the fact that she was almost home, she wasn't sure, and didn't care.

Because it was right in front of her.

The Castle. Gleaming golden in the setting sun, surrounded by green meadows, with the flag flying from the tallest towers.

Celie heard a whoop and turned to look. On one side of her was Lady Griffin. On the other were Pogue and Arrow, who had kept up, and just beyond them were Rolf and Dagger, who had been in the wagon until just a moment ago, she was sure. She grinned fiercely at them all, and then they were sailing over the outer wall and into the courtyard.

Rufus landed with a bump and a scrape right on the front steps.

Celie leaped from his back and ran up the stairs and into the main hall of the Castle. Her Castle. She felt a ripple beneath her feet, and a sensation like the walls were leaning in to embrace her.

"We're back," she shouted. "We're home."

A second later King Glower was there, wrapping his arms around her and crushing her against his velvet tunic. Celie began to sob.

"I'm home," she said. "I'm home."

Acknowledgments

To paraphrase our friend Lulath, I am being so very, O my darlings!

So many people have helped me with this series, and it's been a crazy time. I feel like I've been writing about Castle Glower forever, yet looking back, it's only been a handful of years. Amazing!

So thank you, thank you, to Melanie, Michelle, and Caroline, who came on the first few rides with me! Love you guys! And thank you, thank you, to my current editor, Mary Kate Castellani, who is always a joy to work with, even when I am not. Thanks to Linda Minton, my stellar copyeditor, for keeping track of the names of the people, the griffins, and even the dogs, not to mention reining in my comma usage. A big hug and a thank-you to all at Bloomsbury: Cindy Loh, Cristina Gilbert, Lizzy Mason, Emily Ritter, Erica Barmash, Eshani Agrawal, Hali Baumstein, and Brett Wright. You people are a joy to know!

Huge thanks to my dear friend and agent, Amy Jameson, always there to cheer me on and give me a hand and lend me an ear and feed me delicious food. You are the best!

Enormous hugs and plenty of cake (and pie) for my family, especially my sister, but especially my kids, but ESPECIALLY my husband. Thank you for putting up with me when I am on deadline, because . . . well, I'm always on deadline, and it's never not crazy, and I'm (sort of) sorry.

And last but certainly, CERTAINLY not least, thanks to you, gentle readers. Your enthusiasm for Celie's adventures are what makes my job so fun! You're all brilliant and amazing. I wish I could give you all a very small dog (or a griffin) as a thank-you, but your parents would hate me forever, so I won't!

A GIRL WITH AN ANCIENT
AND FORBIDDEN GIFT...

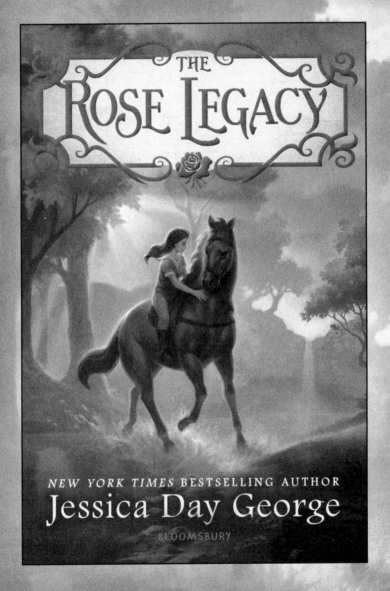

BAD NEWS

ANTHEA BREATHED ON THE cold window, fogging the glass, and wrote her name on the misty pane. *Anthea Genevia Thornley.* Jean, the upstairs maid, would have a devil of a time getting rid of the streaks, but Anthea didn't care. Maybe Jean wouldn't notice, and ever after when the window fogged Anthea's name would reappear.

Anthea had known it would only be a matter of time before she was shunted off to another set of relatives. Nobody wanted her for very long, although they were all very polite about it. It would not have occurred to them not to be, any more than it would have occurred to them to refuse to take her in. And it wasn't as though she were a financial burden: her parents had left her a substantial inheritance. Somehow, though, she always seemed to be in the way.

She had lived with Uncle Daniel and Aunt Deirdre for three years now, the longest she had ever stayed anywhere. But Anthea could see in the frozen expression on Aunt Deirdre's face lately that she was searching for some way to get rid of the unwanted girl.

"A new baby ought to do the trick," Anthea muttered, her breath misting the glass to complete opacity. "At least I don't have to stay on as an unpaid nurse."

One of her mother's cousins had used her as a maid of all work when she was hardly big enough to carry a coal scuttle. Anthea had been more than willing to be "sacked" for her poor silver-polishing skills. After that there was a second cousin whose son had pinched Anthea black and blue until she had slapped him in retaliation . . . and so on and so on.

Uncle Daniel was a dutiful sort who frequently apologized for not taking her in sooner. He had been the ambassador to Kronenhof for most of Anthea's life. But when he had returned to Coronam and the city of Travertine, Anthea had been unceremoniously dumped on his doorstep. Aunt Anne had "put up with" Anthea for nearly a year, she told her brother bitterly, and wasn't about to do it another minute.

"Oooh, Anthea! Jean's going to be so angry with you!"

Anthea turned to see her cousin Belinda Rose standing in the door of the bedroom they shared, her navy skirt and sailor blouse still looking fresh and pressed and her eyes round as she looked at the streaks on the window. Anthea straightened her own blouse and then transferred the frown to her cousin.

"Are you going to tattle?"

"I might," Belinda Rose said in a silky voice. "Or you could do my arithmetic . . ."

Anthea snorted. "I'd rather wash the window," she said, putting her hands to her hips. "Go on and tattle! I'll tell Aunt Deirdre that you were going to cheat."

Belinda Rose put out her lower lip, pouting and thinking at the same time. "Oh, all right!" She flounced off. "Papa wants to see you in the library," she called over her shoulder.

Grumbling, Anthea swatted at her own serge skirt, trying to restore the pleats. She was sure that her cousin had dawdled all the way so that Anthea would be scolded for tardiness.

Downstairs, Anthea knocked on the library door. The leather-upholstered book-filled room was her uncle's sanctuary, and the children were only summoned within when they were in trouble. Which meant that, despite her best efforts, Anthea was summoned to the library at least twice a month.

"Enter."

Anthea took her place on the Kronenhofer rug in front of her uncle's desk. She clasped her hands at her waist and put her shoulders back, head high. She was trying for the exact pose depicted in the portrait of Princess Jennet that hung in the entrance of her school.

Uncle Daniel sat back in his large desk chair, his fingers

steepled under his chin, and studied her. He did not seem impressed. Anthea sagged just a little.

Even though it was highly improper, she spoke first. "Belinda Rose has already told me the news."

"I'm sorry, I didn't want you to hear it from her first." He frowned. "And I must speak to her about tattling."

That gave Anthea a pang, since her cousin had just told her that she would not tattle. But then Anthea sighed, because it didn't matter, really. She would be packed and out the door before Belinda Rose had time to think of a suitable revenge.

"At any rate, Anthea, I *am* sorry about this." Uncle Daniel's face was strained. "It's just that Deirdre and I didn't expect to have any more children. It has come as rather a shock, and necessitated a few . . . adjustments."

"That's all right, Uncle," she managed to say.

She didn't enjoy being lumped into the adjustments, which also included moving a cradle into Elizabeth Rose's room. No one liked feeling like furniture. Anthea didn't comment on that, however, but steeled herself to ask the question that was really troubling her.

"But where will I go? I thought I had exhausted the hospitality of every one of my relations by now."

She grimaced. She didn't mean to be a burden, but since no one wanted her to begin with, they were only too happy to find a reason to get rid of her. It didn't seem to matter how good her grades were, or what awards she won, or how polite and eager to please she was at home. She was an inconvenience no matter what she did.

Her uncle gave her a pained smile. "Yes, er, that's really what I wanted to speak to you about. There is, I'm afraid, only one other option." He straightened the row of silver pencils on his desk. "It was Deirdre's idea, which is surprising . . . ," he muttered.

Anthea crossed her fingers and silently prayed that the only option wouldn't prove to be a spinster aunt who smelled of mothballs and liked to have the death notices in the paper read aloud to her every afternoon.

"You see"—Uncle Daniel cleared his throat and brought her attention back to him—"there really is no flaw in your character. You're an amiable enough young lady, not without looks and charm . . . brains for certain. I wish Belinda Rose had half your . . . but no matter. Your father left you with ample finances as well, and I know you dream of taking up the Rose before you marry . . . a worthy goal indeed." He paused, sighed, pursed his lips, and looked up at the ceiling.

"Then why does no one want me?" The question burst from her lips before she could stop it. She clenched her teeth to stop a sob from following.

Uncle Daniel, to his credit, didn't bother to argue, but looked at her gravely. "Do you know what your father's occupation was?"

The question took her off guard and stopped the tears

before they could fall. "Not really," Anthea admitted. "Actually, not at all."

She had long ago deduced that her father had not been very highly placed in society. After all, everywhere Uncle Daniel went there were men who shook his hand and spoke in reverent tones of his work with the Foreign Office. But never once had Anthea encountered someone who knew her father.

Anthea drew herself up nevertheless and remembered that her mother would never have married someone who wasn't of great importance. Before her marriage, Genevia Cross had been a Favored Rose Maiden. The queen herself had arranged the Cross-Thornley marriage.

"Your father managed his family's estate," Uncle Daniel said, his voice clipped. "It's in a rather . . . unfashionable . . . location. Quite out-of-the-way, one might say."

"His brother, Andrew Thornley, is now the owner. He'll be your new guardian."

"I see."

But she didn't. She had never heard of Andrew Thornley, had not known she had an uncle on her father's side, but Uncle Daniel had begun to speak again.

"He writes that he is thrilled to have you." Uncle Daniel frowned down at a letter on his desk.

Anthea found this highly unlikely; no one was ever thrilled to have her. But it was nice of him to say so. It boded well for the next few months.

"You will leave in two days," Uncle Daniel went on. "Your uncle will meet you at the train station outside the Wall."

"The Wall?" One of her hands rose to the collar of her blouse. "*Kalabar's* Wall? You're sending me to live near the Wall?"

Uncle Daniel rolled his silver pencils beneath his palm. "Not quite. The estate is some distance beyond it, I understand."

Anthea felt the ground heave beneath her feet. Her voice came out as a whisper. "*Beyond* the Wall? In the Exiled Lands?" Her knees were shaking as Uncle Daniel merely gave her a nod in answer.

Without asking permission, Anthea sank down into one of the high-backed leather chairs. The Exiled Lands! That was where the Crown sent traitors, pagans, and other undesirables! She had heard stories from the girls at school who came from northern Coronam. They said that the exiles ate unspeakable things, like raw meat and goat eyeballs. And the women wore trousers while the men wore skirts, but nobody wore drawers at all!

"I'm very sorry."

Her uncle looked sorry. In fact, his face looked lined and almost old, though he was not yet forty. Anthea wondered how much pressure her aunt had put on Uncle Daniel to force him to send his niece into exile. And how dreadful a burden was Anthea that the only option left to her was to be sent into exile herself?

"Is my uncle—my other uncle—is he—" Her throat was so dry she couldn't finish the thought, but Uncle Daniel knew what she was thinking.

"Andrew Thornley is *not* an exile," he said. "He apparently chooses to live there. He says he will explain it to you when you arrive." Uncle Daniel straightened the letter again, his mouth a thin line. "I am so sorry, Anthea. This isn't something I would wish on any young lady of breeding. But I'm afraid that I'm rather at the end of my tether. Deirdre . . ."

He was saved from having to finish that thought by Delia, the downstairs maid, who bustled in, her eyes alight with curiosity. She would be dying to get juicy details about Anthea's banishment she could carry back to the kitchen.

"Dinner is served, sir," she said, her eyes on Anthea.

"Thank you, Delia," Uncle Daniel said sharply.

With a disappointed huff, the maid backed out of the room. She valued her job too much, however, to slam the door or listen at the keyhole.

"You're a good girl, Anthea," Uncle Daniel said. "I'm sure that you'll be all right. In a few years you can look toward a ladies' college of some kind. There are none beyond the Wall, so you will be able to return to Coronam then. You might consider teaching, or nursing."

"Either of those would be nice," Anthea responded dully.

What was running through her head was that all she really wanted was to be a Rose Maiden, like her mother and her aunt

Deirdre. But would the queen select a Maiden who had lived among exiles? Her heart shuddered.

She was ruined.

"Very good," Uncle Daniel said. He seemed relieved, and Anthea realized that, after years of living with Aunt Deirdre, he'd expected her to have hysterics. "You'll be back in civilized society before you know it." He gave her a slight smile. "Anthea?"

"Thank you," she managed.

"You are welcome. You may be excused."

The Long Road North

"OI, REDGE! YOU TOSSER!"

"What? I din't do nuffin!"

"Tha's the point! Mite of a schoolgirl in car two din't get put out at Blackham!"

"I tried! Din't her ticket say the Wall? Din't it just!"

"Cor! Did it?"

"It did! Plain as brass!"

"Never heard th'like. She an exile, then?"

"Too young, in't she?"

"Dunno."

Anthea shut out the conductors' voices with an effort. She opened her book, *Lives of the Crown*, and set it down again. Miss Miniver, the headmistress of her school, had given it to her as a going-away present. In her precise, angular hand the headmistress had written on the frontispiece: *"Let these worthy examples guide you in lawless lands*," but Anthea wasn't in the mood to read stories of piety and sacrifice.

She was restless, but there was nowhere to go, save up and down the narrow aisle of the train. But this activity seemed to be largely favored by men with cigars, and not young ladies, so Anthea didn't dare to try it. Outside the grimy windows, field after field passed by, the monotonous green broken only by a quick glimpse of the occasional town or village. In the beginning there had been frequent stops at bustling stations, with passengers getting on and off and luggage being loaded and unloaded amid gusts of steam from the engine and shouts from the porters.

But everyone in her car had disembarked at the last station, and no one new had gotten on at all. The conductor had been shocked to find her still sitting there and demanded to see her ticket; he was certain that she had forgotten to get off somewhere farther south. There were no more stations left until they reached the Wall, where the train customarily delivered only mail before turning around for the long trek back to the south and civilized society.

Anthea breathed on the window and wrote her name in the foggy patch. Streaking windows with her name would be her way of leaving a mark on the world. Now that it seemed she would have no chance to leave a better one.

If she didn't freeze to death in some hovel, as Belinda Rose gleefully predicted, then her reputation would be ruined. Permanently. Belinda Rose had been sworn to secrecy by her parents, but Anthea knew by the gleam in her cousin's eyes that everyone at Miss Miniver's Rose Academy would know Anthea's fate within a day, a week at the most.

It was dark outside the train now. The green of the fields was gray and black in the moonlight, and Anthea could hardly tell the difference between a barn and a grove of trees. She opened the hamper at her feet and pulled out the last of the sandwiches that Mrs. Murch, Uncle Daniel's cook, had packed for her.

Anthea ate the final sandwich—cold chicken with pickle— and drank the bitter tea. The cake was stale, so she nibbled the icing and candied cherries off the top and left the rest. Then she noticed something sticking out from under the napkin lining the bottom of the hamper. Lifting aside the napkin, she found a letter in what was unmistakably Aunt Deirdre's hand.

Anthea unfolded the note slowly. She wasn't sure she wanted to be treated to a sermon on remembering her place or avoiding foreign customs just now. Something slithered out of the letter and landed in her lap, glinting in the compartment's lamp.

Startled, Anthea looked at it for a long time before she realized that it was a silver pendant on a silver chain. And not just any pendant: a Royal Coronaman Rose, set with a small pearl at its heart.

The Royal Family had ruled Coronam for a thousand years. Princess Jennet, the sister of King Aloster IV, had been the model of all that was good and lovely in a young lady. She had been not only beautiful but intelligent and pious, and so her symbol of the rose had become treasured by all young ladies who aspired to Princess Jennet's example. Jennet had refused to marry so that she might spend her days waiting upon her sister-in-law, Queen Lythia, and had founded the Society of Rose Maidens.

Anthea had always admired the gold-and-garnet rose necklace that Belinda Rose had been given on her last birthday. Anthea set the letter aside and lifted this one. The silver rose was just as finely engraved as her cousin's, and the pearl was a beautiful soft gray, which would suit Anthea's gray eyes. She clasped it around her neck and resolved to try to live up to the example of Princess Jennet, no matter how dire her circumstances.

Then she picked up the letter to read.

My dear niece,

I am so desperately sorry for the grave trial that has been placed before you. But you have always been such a model of gracious behavior that I am sure you shall pass through this time and emerge unscathed, an example to us all.

And remember: if you ever had need of someone to confide in, please confide in me! I will anxiously await all your news.

Your doting aunt,
Deirdre August-Cross, R. M.

JESSICA DAY GEORGE

is the *New York Times* bestselling author of the Tuesdays at the Castle series, the Dragon Slippers series, and the Twelve Dancing Princesses series, as well as *The Rose Legacy*, *Silver in the Blood*, and *Sun and Moon, Ice and Snow*. Originally from Idaho, she studied at Brigham Young University and worked as a librarian and bookseller before turning to writing full-time. She now lives in Salt Lake City, Utah, with her husband and their three children. Her favorite day of the week is Friday because often there is pizza for dinner.

www.jessicadaygeorge.com

@JessDayGeorge

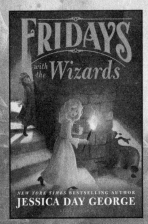